DAYS OF FUTURE FOUND

A NOVEL

M. K. Wark

*To my children and their generation who
still have time to change the world*

CONTENTS

PART ONE

CLIMATE COLONY

CHAPTER 1

ELLA

She ripped off the top of the foil packet, dumping the gray flaky chunks into the hot broth. The escaping odor reminded her of the smell of a new car. New colors and textures came to the surface as she stirred the mixture. Balancing her weight on one leg, she counted. As the boiling pot thickened, she shifted her weight to the other leg. Open on the counter was the one cookbook she allowed herself to keep. A yellowed paper napkin marked the page, a splendid photo of a Mezze dish with dense layers of translucent cucumber, red-purple onion circles, cubed tomatoes, artichoke hearts, and shiny red sweet peppers. Her fingers drifted just above the image as if to summon its delicate essence. For just a moment, her senses traveled back to remember the rich mix of each taste.

The supply of ready-made meal packs sat in tall stacks nearby. The transitions had come about in the last ten years. First, there was scarcity and then the disappearance of most fresh produce. A humbled nation now provided basic nutrition for most of its citizens with rows of soybeans and other protected crops in expansive growhouses. With a cup and a half in her china bowl, Ella moved over to the steel counter. She leaned forward and sipped the end of the spoon. Controlling the consistency helped her avoid the heavy aftertaste of manufactured protein; the traces of the edamame flavor went down smoother as a thinner soup.

At the far end of the counter, a special delivery envelope sat propped up against a box. Last week she ignored two emails and blocked one voice announcement from the Longevity Institute. Then this rare paper bird of a notice landed at her front door. Each day she did not open it, she mentally ripped it to shreds. She was gearing up for a battle, the stakes of which were not clear. An unopened letter was still not news; she could wait until her next dinner with her friend Riley.

Facing her patio window was a broad drab canvas of partly barren hills. On a clear day, she made up cheerful stories of people's lives beyond the protected colonies. The ugly rumors; of new civil unrest had started up again, but they were just that—rumors. Maybe the local security forces made them up to keep citizens homebound and away from potential conflict. Ella wanted to believe in a future where dissent healed itself as an act of self-preservation. They could not go back to choking on its venom. The heavy turmoil was years past, and she knew she was safe here, as safe as anyone can be. She dared not ask for more than to lead a tame life in the corner of a disheveled world.

The cheery voice of the Weather Alert App spoke with its usual authority from the back wall. It confirmed last night's prediction. "Skies will clear by noon. Look for drier moderate temperatures and no immediate threats of an AWE (Acute Weather Event)." Her foot bounced on the chair rung, her mind already moving her body through a busy day. Forecasts were everyone's standard preoccupation. She treated the weather as a moody parental figure, an authority she must reckon, with yet respect. The violent microbursts of rain during the last few years had failed to damage their fortified building. This forecast was a sweet promise. Today the sun will touch down and free her from being a mushroom in a dark, damp corner.

Outside, rolling gray blankets pulled back to show a sad, pale blue sheet streaked with scratchy white clouds. She was set for a feel-good buffet of gentle breezes and steady warmth on her hands and face and a checklist of things to do outside. A sunny day helped her push back from those 'back then' thoughts. Thinking too much about the loss of going where you wanted, when you wanted, did not get you anywhere at all. The daydream often came back. She was wandering through a clothing store, an old habit during the last years of a stressful job. It was her retail relaxation therapy. In those days, she spent hours sorting through racks of clothes to find a unique bargain, a simple exercise to calm a worried mind. Today was a chance to wear her mix-matched relics and flaunt being a curiosity. She was in the middle of the new old age, too old to be an aging millennial, too young to be a very old boomer.

Ella opened her narrow closet, crossed her arms, resenting the amount of space the eco suit took up. Like a stiff disembodied scarecrow, it dangled there with too many zippers and loose pieces of Velcro. Citizens were provided with the standard-issue multi-temperature eco-protection suits for the seasons, reliable protection but not much to say for style or color. They kept you dry in wild rain, warm in the chilling cold and a few degrees cooler when the heat was the relentless enemy. She elbowed it to the far side, smacking it top to bottom as if dismissing an opponent in martial combat. After a slow relaxing breath in and out, she straightened back up and reached farther back into the space. The tips of her fingers stroked the worn smoothness of the padded satin hanger, lingering down and across the wild floral embroidery of a linen blouse. She pulled it off, then bunched it up, and pressed it to her chest for a momentary hug. Even with the missing buttons and the fuzzy threads on the cuffs, it was a prize. It once belonged to her older sister, and it tipped her mood to a peaceful place.

Stepping over to the Local Conditions Display near the patio wall, she tapped the power screen. The rows of LED lights —-red, —-orange, —- yellow, —-green —-flashed and danced across the gauge quizzing the outside air quality. It was like waiting for a casino slot machine to roll a quadruple bar combination. Green was the winner today. The vacuum seal on the patio door hissed its distinct pop-sucking sound. Next to the glass panel, she paused a moment and closed her eyes and sorted out her rarified inside existence from the clutch of raw natural elements that lurked outside. The dank air thrust in. When she did not smell particulate in the air, she took in a deep breath. There was no nuclear war, no mass killing virus. The steady encroachment of constant erratic weather and multiple natural disasters coupled with the old neglect of pollution controls made breathing a daily exercise in trust that things were better. Her memory rewound to a time when opening the door on her old deck came with a crazy chorus of manic chirps and twerps of birds and chipmunks. Right now, she tried to block out the ugly crunching sound of the grounds keeping equipment below.

She stepped over the metal threshold onto her tiny oasis; this barely-there triangular balcony allowed her outside time on temperate days. By her own choice, she deeded her old house with a full yard to the cause of making babies. New residents were enjoying its ample room to grow a family; she still had this postage stamp of outdoor space with her unit. Layers of others lived above, below, and beside her, compressing her into an area less than her old living room. The small patio showed proof of her steely determination to grow a minimalist garden. The pepper plants grew under purple lights on her side of the window most of the time. With the long spells of rain bombs, gray days of spring and the bruising sunshine of the summer, the lights allowed a predictable substitute. Today she would treat them to some partial sun. California Red Wonder peppers used to be the name.

She preserved the seeds each year with care. The peppers were never as red or as large, but their stalks and spindly leaves held fast lashed to supports. These plants were a fragile promise that a growing summer would come again. With a decent crop, she swapped them for other rare goods at the common market.

She pulled the straps on the plant dollies and rolled them outside. Few citizens wasted a portion of their power allotment on trying to grow personal plants. Placing them against the railings, Ella checked the health of the leaves and the dampness of the soil. Watching and waiting for signs of new growth always fueled her gardener's optimism.

Stepping back, Ella caught sight of her neighbor waving from the opposite balcony. She smiled again, knowing she was lucky to have Olivia and her husband, Fred, so close. They were positive mood people, and why not? The touchstones of their cheerfulness, their daughter with two young ones, lived in the immediate area. They never lacked for visitors and hugs.

Olivia called out across the courtyard, "Hi Ella, looks like a walking weather day for you."

"Grandkids coming over on lunch break?" Ella shouted back. Olivia nodded and put her hands to her heart. "We have new neighbors moving in on the third-floor level. I hear they are young couples, which is great."

Ella made an openhanded gesture, "Yes, but what happened to the older couple and the widow? It seemed sudden."

Olivia just shook her head in agreement and then put her hands up in the air as if to say, who knows? Behind her, Fred maneuvered his walker towards the open balcony door one foot-plant at a time. She watched his labored progress and leaned over her railing as if to draw him closer. While she waited, a broad smile never left his face.

"Good afternoon," he chanted as if welcoming a grand crowd before him. "The grandkids are meeting me at the picnic tables to play chess. Still learning the moves - smart ones you know," he announced with an even wider grin. Fred radiated a kind of 'I am still here and have reasons to be happy about it' attitude.

Ella gave Fred double thumbs up. She lived in a time when all children were prizes in a rigged lottery. The New Education was teaching the new young ones to believe they could mold their future into a better one than what came before and not repeat the mistakes of the past. Running into those two, ages seven and nine, was a rare occasion but it jump-started her day. The pair rushed by but left a gentle storm of happy noise and positive energy in their wake. They were new age babies, born after years of mass infertility. Olivia had confided to Ella that the children were confused about their place in history. Anyone who lived through the sour political unrest and then the payment due of climate change had to make a decision. You believed either that sacrifices had to be made in the present to preserve some part of the future or you went your way without regulated shelter and protection. You either bowed to technology and order or took your chances and dropped off the radar. Ella participated in the movement with a firm desire for stability to force fundamental change through Voters Voice. She had lived long enough to watch both extremes in worldview melt off the spectrum from sheer weariness.

Just talking to Olivia and Fred about the grandchildren was a tonic. They knew the seeds of hopefulness were sprouting again in the minds of the next generation. Ella calculated her own cautious stock in the future. She had been able to work longer than most at something she loved to do - programming. Problem solving in little bits of code was a challenge that many people did not aspire to. Some of her work skillsets had been hijacked by advancing AI. That part of her brain was not in demand any longer. Now with only part-time assignments doing minor software revisions and creating positive thought e-cards for her old company, she was grateful to have a small current of creativity flow into an otherwise staid existence. Those were her pluses.

All the bad stuff about the loss of her husband and family, she tucked away.

She turned back into the unit and avoided walking close to the counter. The letter from the Institute arrived two days ago. She had joined the biological age challenge study back when she was in her mid-forties. Somehow, now twenty years later, she was outpacing others her age even by the new standards of what defined healthy aging. What other parts of her blood, genes, and chromosomes did they want to examine now? Why was she aging at 'half-speed'? The Institute fixated on something on the tips of her DNA. She believed in the advancement of the new aging science. The irony was that the world was battered and barren from the ravages of climate yet those who stuck to the diet, supplements, and exercise routine were staying around longer. Their labs couldn't explain why her telomeres on her DNA were not fraying. She had looked online to understand more and stared at the illustrations. The answer as to why she still had the stamina and mental agility of a younger person was some-how inside those Q-tip like structures. Early on, the Longevity lab people had shared with pride an image of her DNA. All she saw were two-headed caterpillars with bright lights on both ends. Her aging was no longer a personal thing, rather a spectator sport. Having her anatomy mined for a profit point was not okay.

She grabbed her left wrist covering the small blinking screen. Maybe it was time for a small-scale revolt. Releasing the triple clasp, she threw the Life Bit on the countertop. Taking a tiny screwdriver, she loosened the battery compartment just enough so that it emitted a change battery signal. With a measure of defiance and mischief, she dropped it into a tall piece of lead-glazed pottery. As she looked down into the bottom, the constant scrolling of tiny red and blue hearts was now purple.

Let that confuse them for a while. A few hours lapse would not set off alarms and send people to her door. She had bargained for extra scrutiny and innovations to stay younger healthier longer by becoming a walking, sitting, sleeping meter reader of her excellent health span.

This letter can't be just another simple invitation to a seminar pep rally for the living longer crowd. Maybe the researchers found something marketable in her latest bio samples. Her friend Riley has been telling her all along it was naive to think she was safe from the turmoil in the world. Riley believed there were other negative forces out there. She came here to be secure, and now she was turning into a frightened lab rat, tired of the maze but too scared to take her chances out there where routine and order meant so little. Having a regular income and protected housing was no small accomplishment for any citizen. Those who chose to avoid the new order lived not as pioneers but as scavengers continually moving to meet their needs.

Ella pulled the shades back, glanced out past the mountains, and then drifted out again onto the patio. Riley was on the road today as a bike courier. She envied her friend's lack of fear in moving freely beyond the colony. Today she would be content with her familiar path in the community. Riley had made it a regular habit to stoke fear in her to match her paranoid view. The information she gathered on her trips outside their protected space always pointed to not trusting that their lives were their own or that the new order was working for everyone. For months now, Ella had been able to temper Riley's observations and growing paranoia with common sense. Nevertheless, it was a battle that neither side seemed to be winning. Ella tilted her head, fussed over the plants, and turned them to the softness of the growing sunshine. She trimmed the weakest leaves to make the new growth stronger. It was a constant effort to banish the old ghosts of personal loss; they were creeping up on her again. She stabbed at the air as if to use the handy tool to dismiss the past from recasting her life into another drama of loss and grief. Letting go, she dropped the snips back into her gardening bag.

It was a simple promise; I will not box myself into a bad thought corner right now. The gift of an outside afternoon is mine to enjoy.

* * *

LIFE Database Control Center - 4.14.2039 – 12:37 EST
Location Climate Colony #42
Subject: Ella D 540 752-O

Change in algorithms key a check/respond alert: Send message: Bio-Genome Harvest Project: Priority 1 B status
TECH #1

"Do we need to respond to change in status?"
TECH #2

"No, she has done this before. She will be back after taking 20,000-25,000 steps, make three to four stops and two to three purchases."
TECH#1

"Allow no vitals until return but double-check face recognition and debit card at Horti-culture base #15 and FM#23. We can't let her wander off. She has too much potential."
TECH #2

"They think they are slipping the bonds of earth, but only for a while."

* * *

RILEY

Riley stared off to her right, searching for the best spot to pull over. Air-filled her lungs as the muscles in her thighs and calves grew numb from the push to make the last few miles. Twisted bikes and other debris on the side of the highway mounded together in piles. In this stark jumbled landscape, she hoped no poachers would notice if she left the main road. Her bike's solar cell could do a fast re-charge, grabbing some of the sun's fleeting glo-ry. Other travelers continued past her to the next rest stop. They would take their breaks in the outdoor canteen. She needed a spot just far enough off the road to recharge the bike's battery and her flagging stamina.

A massive gray boulder halfway up the hill caught her eye. As she paused on the shoulder and waited, two other bikers and a scooter passed before she pushed up the embankment. The soggy ground grabbed the wheels as they rolled over the forest floor. No leaves, just debris and fallen twigs caught in the spokes and treads. She lifted her leg and swung it to the ground in a measured way to prevent her hip from screaming out in pain. Off came the heavy helmet. A scant breeze met the light sweat on the back of her neck and the matted, purple hair on the top of her head. She looked around and decided this was her spot; that she could get away with napping out in the open even with scavengers out there.

The electric bike frame folded as she laid it on the ground, the photovoltaic cells pivoted to claim maximum exposure. She wrapped the long bungee cord around the boulder and through the spokes of the wheels and pulled the camouflage tarp out of her pack, spread it out and sunk in slow motion to the ground. She placed her extra jacket as a pillow, curled up in a fetal position, and yanked the rest of the tarp over herself and the bike.

The best part of this job was being outside when the weather was not wretched. Staying fit and biking had been second nature in her younger years. A day like this now required a real effort to push back against a serious energy drain that pulled her towards sleep. She had tried all the population-tested supplements for her age group, but none of them provided the boost she needed. Her friend Ella, a decade-plus older, could handle this trip better. She bent down to massage away the steady throb in both her knees. Like a hand-wound clock that keeps stalling and losing time, she was too young to be decelerating. Riley had willed her legs to stay steady and not revolt. Today's assignment was only a fifty-mile round trip to deliver confidential jump drives on an electric-powered glide bike. Others her age did not find these assignments so demanding.

The courier gig came with some interesting coding work. She was lucky to have this hybrid job. The real danger was being outside the protected colonies and not having reserve strength to deal with the fringe element. There were city-states with order and laws and states with their own version of law and order. Those who didn't want to be part of the new system made life on their own as nomadic tribes in secluded places. Like herds, they wandered looking for the next best grazing place. They did not want rules that kept you safe, fed, and housed. No government was going to tell them where to live. The truth had somehow become the enemy of freedom.

On the open road, she faced the real threat of IT pirates seeking ransom for the worthy contents of a courier's pouch. Riley somehow relished this threat with her usual measure of reckless over-confidence. It is what made life exciting right now. Why not this space beside this boulder? With only the photovoltaic cell exposed, she was just another piece of the litter on the hill. Being out on the highways was different now; personal passenger cars were scarce. Bikes and scooters, self-driving cars and delivery vans made up most of the traffic on scarred, bumpy roads.

She squirmed, stretched, and tried to make her right hip mesh into the pockmarked face of the hill. The slow, gnawing pain stopped as she settled. This morning she had taken some of the newer, non-addictive pain meds. The pills allowed only a fraction of relief, but overuse of any prescribed drugs would bring attention she did not want. Riley knew her bio stats were not keeping up with the new longevity/vitality scales. In a longevity-enhanced world, she was on the other side of that. There were no accidents or family illnesses in her past — no arthritis on her scans, no known immune disorders. For whatever reason, she was aging a lot quicker than expected.

She tucked the pouch next to her rib cage, and arranged the tarp one more time and wondered about the proprietary rating on this bunch of drives. The hacking of both government and corporate information had spawned a new era of data sharing protections. She had a job because on the local level authorities relied on the bike couriers to deliver large numbers of Nano terabyte drives. They could outsmart an ambush better than a self-driving vehicle that could be hacked. If these files were a high priority, the pouch would implode if anyone tampered with the lock. Her employer issued a firearm for travel, but incidents were rare. The road pirates knew that taking a courier's pouch would mean the destruction of the contents and part of their anatomy.

She finally had a job she wanted after over two decades of just getting by. Why did her generation always have to compromise in terms of jobs and careers? Three decades ago, the recession kicked the crap out of opportunities even for college grads. Riley felt caught between the new and old order of things, like a spider caught in its web.

Along with her peers, the nagging lack of financial security intensified her will to make changes. It was like setting a metronome in motion with the speed increasing. Twenty years ago, she was an active part of a movement that pushed to reinvent government, as you would create a new cocktail experimenting with the mix of ingredients until you got it right. In a steady push from election to election, she was there to protest, organize, and motivate others. Take a threatened democracy, stir in benign socialism of necessity and add a garnish of capitalism lite. Her age group stood and delivered the political will and votes to no longer be dismissed and disenfranchised. They were a real force behind transforming the societal order to work for the majority, not the privileged minority. It was not a revolution for the impatient, but Riley knew she was one of the most impatient people alive.

Today she had her agenda on top of three deliveries. Once she reached the port area, she wanted to check things out for herself. It had started with rumors and shady online conspiracy theories that lacked hard evidence. Then she had overheard someone talking about his or her grandparents taking a secret cruise then never coming back. There were still a couple of big boats in the harbor. She had formed her new cause. The question was why in this modern, improved society with all its advances in longevity and medical cures, were more and more of its oldest and most impaired citizens evaporating from sight? She set the safety on her weapon, put it at a hand's length and again checked the position of the tarp. The wrist alarm would rouse her in fifty minutes. The soothing low hum of the charging unit pressed softly into her head as she dropped off to sleep.

* * *

ALVI
Alvi placed the caution cones at equal intervals along the entryway and kicked on the vacuum in the lower patio area. The debris on the upper exterior corridors would have to wait. She wanted to make sure the giant orange machine lumbered back and forth across the pavement in the correct preprogrammed pattern. Robo tech was something she never entirely relied on, so direct supervision was in order. The bulbous hippo made sucking, growling noises loud enough to annoy all the residents in the units above. Shredded pieces of old plastic containers blown in from last night's storm disappeared from the walkway. Keeping the external areas clear was a grunt task and just

part of the job that was always available, but no one wanted. She enjoyed the sense of controlling everything by bits and pieces. Monitoring the power grid, managing the accounting for income dispersal, grounds beautification, and people skills all came under this job description- colony caretaker. This job was the best she could do for now and still keep up with her post-14th-grade classes. It was a stepping stool, if not a ladder, to secure work life.

Taking command of the small space, she performed her menial duties like a fierce warrior going to battle. When the vac sputtered on the turnaround, she met it with another kick and a threatening glare that warned it to behave. As if it read her emotions, the machine lurched back on course. Alvi followed it through another two turns. There must be adherence to rules. Things must go by the book. She learned at an early age that the goal of forging a different future for herself and others her age required discipline. Satisfied that the vac could be trusted to complete its task on the walkways, Alvi ducked into her studio unit. She stood, arms crossed and leaned over the desk to read the mail app. There were several personal messages from friends, in memes and gifs, inviting her to a three-day weekend. Her heavy school assignments were lining up as usual. No requests for repairs or replacement parts nagged at her. The semi-decent weather forecast permitted some outdoor plans. It looked promising. The power grids were functioning smoothly, and her residents chill for the most part. The decision to go or stay and just study was hers.

This assignment came with the right mix of residents. Sweet Ella worked online doing creative things. The older couples on the mid-floors were self-sufficient and generally very approachable. The younger couples and Riley were always busy with their jobs. Her only real worry was the elderly gentleman who lived on the top deck right. She was still trying to make sense of his behavior, even after months of being the colony's caretaker. Harold skipped all the escorted social activities for the older residents. Full Pharma had perfected pain amelioration for arthritis and other old age ills without the mind-numbing addiction. Why would it be a pain thing? There were no major acute medical problems in his records, and he remained independent and self-sufficient. To observe and report on the older residents was one part of her function. Longevity enhancement was now an established science, calculated for maximum comfort and prolonged independence. As individuals fail, there were other arrangements that she did not want to know about. Her job was to keep her residents ahead of that decision as long as possible.

Alvi logged the deliveries to all the residents, confirming that Harold never lacked in the usual necessities. Months ago, she helped his CCR (Closest Concerned Relative) with permits to add some impressive assistive equipment to his unit. She found herself repeating her training mandate to herself. You cannot enforce socialization, only encourage it. Somehow, she knew this older man was going to make her assignment more difficult. Most elders were grateful for the interventions and entertainment that she offered.

Her gerontology classes had taught her to look for more in his history. Ella shared that Harold was a former choirmaster or a musician. Maybe tickets to a hologram concert (a rare treat for anyone) or at least a rental for a VR GO headset to take a 3D trip back to a concert would help. Her training infused her with the tenet that aging is a natural process. Like the final movement of a long, intricate symphony, you know it is coming, and at a certain point, you must let the notes play out. That particular professor tended to be somewhat passionate as he drilled down on the concept. He predicted that with older age being a third of your life, attitudes would change.

Change was all she had known. School for her and her older sister began in chaotic times. She came home crying because of the awful words thrown at her. The country where she was born was not her country. Then it was everyone's country to save. As she and her older sister matured, they watched a thin thread of optimism woven into a collective fiber to adapt and conquer the threats of climate and the storm of social change. She also grew up with the good stuff. Cures for major diseases rained down as managed state-to-state migration spared many from disaster. Alvi expected a new pill or techno invent, or a current law would appear when needed, but then everyone must obey the rules.

After reading her email, she looked into the account distribution software to check on the colony income credits and found a positive balance in the unity fund. Last summer, she had procured glossy green PVC trees and shrubs for the exterior of the building with a well-managed lottery win. The manufactured greenery diverted attention from the stark gray concrete surface. She coveted the compliments. Her colony looked less like a phalanx of defense shields on stilts and more like a low budget public garden. She searched online to see what else was available in the colony co-op catalog. Maybe she could buy some additional bolt-down benches for the shared patio space. She liked the green ones with the fancy scrollwork.

Alvi turned to her log sheets and put in brief but positive remarks regarding the comfort and independence of each of the older residents for the last week. Her previous job assignment drained her, having to document the considerable decline in a group of nonagenarians, but it built up some emotional grit. She bounced back out onto the central patio and picked up the cones and remoted the vac to its cubby in the storage area. Riding up in the external glass elevator to complete the final sweep on the top deck, she stared into each of the residents' patio windows. As the elevator cab pulled into the top floor, she noticed Harold tapping on the ceiling above him with his cane.

"Damn ...it," Alvi cursed and sighed aloud at the same time. "There is no one above him." She made a mental entry for her roster. Maybe a psych eval was in order.

* * *

HAROLD

He wrapped his left hand around the edge of the dining counter as firmly as he could.

Following the strains of the music blasting from his audio feed, he lifted his right hand and stroked the air with his cane. As the grand choral piece gave him new energy, Harold closed his eyes. He imagined his chorus of talented singers before him and the adoring public behind. This was a recording of one of his last concerts. It transported him back forty years to a comfortable corner of his life. The steady applause washed over him, far better than any mood-enhancing pill. He had rejected many medications for various maladies along the way to becoming this old. Why change the focus of the lens when your vision was clear? Part of a dwindling generation that had always enjoyed indulgence to their wishes, he still had part of his social security check and some savings on top of the public income credits, this unit, and his privacy. It was a better situation here, while others lived in basic public housing. No one would go without the basics, but some older citizens still had private assets.

He ambled with care over to the bathroom and looked at the heat indicator. The shower enclosure program was set to his comfort level. He undressed with effort and removed the headphone/receiver amplifier piece from around his better ear. The tile coils heated the walls, and the floors as the room became a giant down comforter. The advanced technology used earlier for individuals who use wheelchairs allowed him to stand by the shower seat that extended out, and sit with help from the roll bar. Once he was safe on the bench, the sensor pulled him gently back into the shower stall. He jacked up the wall speakers as the next section of his playlist proceeded on cue and in harmony. Like a clam inside a protected habitat, he settled in to enjoy being separate and serene. With the controls in front of him, like a pilot in a cockpit, he started the hot mist stream that released soap and shampoo. With a deep sigh, he rubbed his sinewy feet against the rotating loofah/brush. No bars of soap to drop, everything was within his limited reach. He skipped undoing his ponytail as getting it back together was cumbersome. He would be clean enough for today's standards and grateful for this careful comfort. Harold accomplished his sweet soothing independent ritual of water and music every other day.

His grandnephew Colin arranged to push the electricity credit allocation towards maintaining this bathroom environment with less towards his food prep. He was an infrequent visitor, but they connected once a week on People Time. As the only remaining family in his shrinking world, Colin took extra care of the small details in Harold's life that helped him stay independent. He sent his clothes out for alterations, so dressing was easier and ordered more prepared meals that appealed to Harold's waning sense of taste. It all mattered. The best gift of all was this personalized playlist of precious music that accented each part of his day.

Harold slouched in the seat after the water stopped and let the gentle heat of the drying mechanism do its job. After the next movement of the symphony, he pushed the rocker switch to bring him back out into the room. His change of clothes was there, his loud boxers, grandpa jeans and an even bolder Hawaiian shirt with snaps. After the time in the hot penetrating moisture, his augmented joints slipped back in time. He pulled up his jeans and retrieved his cane. His bare feet slipped into his worn moccasins.

He ambled over to the kitchen area. He must eat a perfunctory late breakfast and keep to a decent meal schedule. The scale built into the bathroom floor (he conceded on that point to Colin) would give him away if he went down too far down in his weight. He did not want any blowback. He heard the weather app pledge a pleasantly dry, warmish interlude for today and tapped the unit as if to question its validity. It would be good to go out to the common area and let others take note of his existence. Being out there, he felt like an exotic hothouse orchid sitting on a greenhouse shelf, admired amid the constant point of speculation as to the time left before the petals fall. His six-inch silver-white ponytail, the exotic floral shirts were jolts of color and soft fabric throwbacks to another time. He was a sight to see in this gray-brown world. Looking down from his patio window, he calculated how long it would take him to walk the length of the corridor, ride down the elevator and over to the stone benches. His scooter sat up against the far wall. Now thin as a walking stick, it was too intimidating. He could find many reasons to pass on the relative rewards of an outside day. His time to leave would come soon enough.

CHAPTER 2

Ella paced back over to the massive glass panel and looked over her plants one more time as if to pull the soft sunlight back into her unit. She wrapped an old hiking jacket around her waist. It was the habit of a weather skeptic. A promise of consistent weather was just that, only a promise. She locked her front door and almost skipped down the walkway to the elevator. Once on the ground level, she waved to young Alvi. Ella already knew the frame of the coming conversation, and it rarely tipped over into something spontaneous.

"Good day to be outside," the young woman's tone was so controlled that Ella imagined it was coming out of a Cylinder Companion, crisp and even in its delivery. She knew it was best to respond to Alvi's authoritative tone in an equally calm and clear pitch. She did not want to appear manic as if escaping the prison yard. The young woman's powers of observation were intense. Ella felt the warm blush spread across her cheeks. She hoped Alvi would record it as a sign of good health and not attribute it to a racing pulse. In a measured tone, she said,

"Yes, I hope they have some newer items at the common market."

She had lived through six of these two years at a time caretakers. This one was at least more positive and less intrusive. For better or worse, they do not last. Alvi did not make her feel like there was another agenda going on. These units were highly prized new-age real estate that could withstand severe storms and provide personal safety. The last caretaker had been caught taking bribes to move out some of the older residents.

Ella stepped on the swept surface at the beginning of the pedestrian path. Like Dorothy in the Wizard of Oz, her adventure was ahead but without the yellow brick road and munchkins to shepherd her along the way. She dismissed the idea of taking a scooter, an electric bike, or a jitney. The two-mile round trip to the Colony Center gave her the real reward of walking with her thoughts.

Couch potatoes simmered in hours of audio/visual distraction in this remade world. In the colony units, everyone had access to an extensive digital viewing library. Her favorite programs were the legacy National Parks and travel shows. Vast serene places of natural beauty were now condensed to multiple digital formats. Every movie ever made was free, courtesy of the BCE (Bureau of Culture and Entertainment). Volumes of old formula dramas and cop shows were available for those who wanted to dig or wallow in the entertainment graveyards of the past.

During the last AWE, she pulled up her favorite opera piece and ignored the persistent howl of the windstorm. She wrapped herself in Pavarotti's deep baritone and marveled at the expansion of his lungs singing La Nostra Dame. The sheer power of the performance always brought her to tears, if not always to peace. Now on this long walk to the Colony Center, her mind examined and judged her balanced present with emerging worries about an uncertain future.

Her steady brisk pace, straight posture and mop of silver hair elicited a few shy smiles along the way. She felt like a walking poster adult. If the Longevity Institute had a catalog, there she would be, smiling her blissful smile with the caption: "Female, early-sixties, with the stamina and endurance of a forty-five-year-old." The wrinkles were still there, yet the testing has proven that she was not losing on biomarkers in the usual categories. She had the stamina, both physical and mental, of someone much younger. Being flexible and agile seemed more like a right than a gift until she encountered others her age. She had followed the Institute guidelines and taken the supplements. Gratitude for the extra encouragement to live a long healthy life had now turned into a nagging intrusion. She read the reports; how do you get excited about lysosomal activity or cellular senescence? She wanted her whole life to be more than the sum of her coveted biomarkers. Trying to shake off those thoughts, she looked along the border of the path. A direct encounter with a family is what she wanted; it was a sport, like trying to spot a rare species in the wild.

Ella married young, lost her husband to random gun violence, and suffered the loss of her only niece to the last of the opioid epidemic all within one year. As the youngest of her sibs, she felt the sour sting of being the last survivor. It was scribbled on her reports in the margin, 'elder orphan,' a status that gave her priority and protection in legal representation and financial guardianship. She was taking better care of herself because she had no one left to care for.

Sometimes a calmer belief won her over. Maybe this entire bio mumbo jumbo meant there was more for her ahead. She knew the effort to patch over the hole in her soul with a quilt of realism and optimism was still a work in progress. Most days, she chose the optimistic part by remembering common sense had taken over to build a new platform for the public good. Ella granted her house and property without bitterness to a young couple with three small ones. She liked to imagine all the good times that the young family was having in her old house. It was a commonly held belief that any couple, who could handle the re-engineering of basic procreation and assisted fertility, deserved priority for owning the remaining single-family homes. She had ample time to pack her more personal possessions. The little unit here in the climate colony was a coveted piece of real estate.

Unable to have children early in her marriage, she watched the incredible medical advances come too late for her as she entered her late-forties. Then, the world suffered a tsunami of infertility on a massive scale. Insect borne diseases and other pollutants ravaged the hormones of a population weakened by climate challenges. For a time, her own barren sorrow was every other involuntary infertile woman's nightmare. For most of a decade, the youngest generation was missing. The line graph of the population growth looked like a waterfall followed by a bubbling stream trying to come back to life.

Without the usual spring critter sounds, she had to fight the sensation of walking through an old graveyard. Each side of the path held the mummified remains of fallen trees. April was now just an extension of the winter without the extreme cold temperatures. She slowed her pace as she got to her first goal of the day, the park commons. In the middle sat a geodesic glass dome. She fancied it as a giant glistening clear crystal Christmas ornament cut in half and screwed into the ground. Ella approached the dome with a measured reverence and holding in her enthusiasm for what she hoped to see.

A lone specimen of a cherry tree in early bud grew inside. On the old almanac calendar, it should be spring. Two decades ago, she would be cleaning up after the fallen glory of the flowering trees in her yard. She crossed her arms and studied all the minute details of the changes and growth since last week. A few petals have started to unfold and reveal their true pink and white touches with a reddish throat almost defiant as if they knew they couldn't be blown away or chilled out by an angry atmosphere. Other walkers gathered around the circumference of the dome. They pointed in a mirror image to those on the other side. Cameras mounted high on the enclosure took in the whole crowd but lingered on her for just a moment.

There was a posted notice; there would be a walkway of pavers around the tree inside the dome by the end of summer so small groups could enter. Two workers sprayed an outline on the cultivated ground soil. For now, fake daffodils and artifact bird sounds supplemented the whole effect. The glory was that the tree was real, healthy, and a major accomplishment of retro-horticulture. Ella lingered. With the generous new maternity/paternity policies, parents often hung around with their precious progeny.

As she stood close to the glass, she felt a gentle tug at her pant leg. She looked down to see a small smog mask nestled in the curls of a child of about two or three. Her pulse jumped. He was grinning up at her with his pale face and pointing to the blossoming tree.

"...uzzy tree!...uzzy tree!" She did not move, knowing this little one would have someone watching him. A uniformed nanny was right behind them.

"Come here, Edward, we can look at the tree from back here." He held on to her pant leg, so Ella pivoted slowly, and with her most sincere smile, leaned down and said: "Aren't you so smart?"

"Yes, this one is always two steps ahead of me."

The nanny did not scoop him up and hurry off. She allowed the child to lead Ella back to a bench, and they all sat together with the child in the middle.

"You know he is not mine, just minding him. Just got here three years ago, lost our house and everything but this work is good ...and he is a good boy."

Ella listened to the nanny and guessed the accent, Arkansas, Oklahoma...one of the devastated states? She paid polite attention to a tale she has heard many times before, a sudden evacuation with losing/leaving everything. Maybe it was something about the soft kindness in her face that people knew she would listen. Ella figured the woman was in her late forties as the tale took the familiar form of a three-act play, losing what they owned, relocating, and a fresh struggle to start over.

"They re-trained my husband, taught him to be a wind/solar tech helper. The math in school almost fried his brain, but I am so proud of him, worry about him falling though. Sure beats what he did before..."

Ella made intermittent eye contact and nodded, "Sounds like things are better for you now."

The nanny went on, "Yeah, I work three different family assignments. This little guy is the best part of my week. So many questions from this one..."

Ella glanced over at the woman as she talked while the activity of the child beside her had the strength of a magnet.

"Our daughters are almost done their schooling now, trying to figure out what they can do. It's a whole new world..."

As she kept pace and responded to each beat of the woman's story, Ella delighted in absorbing the freshness of this curious creature. Suddenly the child climbed right over on to her lap and faced her. His weight made Ella sit up straighter and brace herself against the back of the bench. The nanny did not skip a beat in her tale; she slipped off her shoes and rubbed her bare feet on the artificial turf.

Ella enveloped the child's warm bare hands in hers to help him balance. She treated them like tiny pillows made of sweet dough that needed just the right amount of pressure. He squirmed and then settled down in her lap like a bird burrowing in a nest. She wanted to freeze this moment while she studied the sweetness of his delicate features. He stared at her blouse. His fingers traced the outline of the frayed but still bright colors of the embroidery.

He looked up at her and declared,

"...uzzy flowers." He concentrated a while longer, and then said,

"Did you grow these?"

Ella let out a slight laugh, "No, someone sewed them."

"What is z...ewed?"

A raucous tone sounded from the nanny's phone. She jumped up, retrieved her shoes, and took the child by the hand.

"Edward, time for us to go back." Another minute and they were gone.

Ella leaned forward from the hard bench and let her arms dangle out to the front. She was as close to giddy as she had been in a long while. The child's enthusiasm was contagious. Maybe the world still contained a measure of innocence with unspoken possibilities ahead. She absent-mindedly looked past the next few passersby with a vacant smile. From a distance, she spotted two other sets of young ones. Twins, they were the product of the advanced IVF; one boy-one girl, the new equalitarian way to start and finish a family. The intimacy of sharing space with one so young was still casting a spell. She scraped together

her thoughts as she rose from the bench. Bit by bit, light and dark, they fell away as she headed further down the path.

Off to the side, she saw the OPEN TODAY sign. A tattered hand-painted cloth banner was strung across the top of the wide doors of an old barn. Ella let out a sad chuckle. This 'Farmer's Market' was beyond recognition for those old enough to remember what that name meant. She hesitated to leave the trail of the sun outside, but this stop was a part of her routine, so she shook off her daydreaming. Entering the building was always a familiar trip back in time like going down the same road with familiar signposts. Inside, she glanced up at the newer concrete reinforced beams that somehow blended with the quaintness of the original structure. Every part of the structure was reinforced for protection from the relentless weather changes. The well-done blend of wood beams and concrete bone arched over her like a cathedral. She inspected the well-worn display cases. A security camera followed her as she dug among the dry, dusty books and a few odd pieces that had drifted in here from the previous lives of strangers. They were unique in their own right, but she pushed them aside. They were other people's legacies, not hers. People still wanted those old

LP covers for decoration. The vinyl had been recycled into bowls. A constant visual litany of deceased rock groups sat side by side on the counter, Morrison, Jaeger, Joplin, Prince, and Bowie. Many died young; others had seemed to live forever, but all had left a legacy.

Ella took her time testing her memory and cataloged in her mind what was new and what had been removed. It was like more a museum than a store. Weary from that, she stepped over to the produce section with anticipation. At least sometimes, that offered a pleasant surprise. The post hydroponic garden people were both relentless and diligent, always attempting to cultivate something fresh, edible, if not super tasty. There was always kale to buy. Today they had several climate hardy varieties, Tuscan, Siberian, Red Winter and Dwarf Blue, each with their subtle differences in green to blue color and delicate curliness. She welcomed an approving nod of recognition from the growers behind the counter; after all, she was the red pepper lady.

"Hey Ella, how's your crop coming along?" Burt, the youngest of the growers, teased her, "Still using the old dirt the old way? You need to come to learn with us. You have the touch..."

"Tell me when you're growing real tomatoes and I will," Ella quipped. They were too young to know the sweet, pungent smell of a tangle of real tomato plants. He handed her back the debit card and the kale. He looked twice at her card as he gave it back. "Your card is sparkling extra today, Ella. You are our best customer."

As they chatted, Ella ran her fingers across the bottom of the curly kale leaves on the counter, and then brushed the delicate dill with the back of her hand. She knew she could get away with touching the plants. The growers always coveted a few of her prized red peppers to sit out on the counter. The shiny reddish beacons helped to draw buyers over to their stall. Whatever less than perfect plants they nurtured, she always took some home. The carrots were stubby, the cabbages small as baseballs. She stood there a moment longer, pushing her recall to the sensory delight of being in a fully stocked organic produce section and inhaling a flood of mixed freshness. Then the acrid dampness inside the old reinforced barn brought her back to reality.

Ella started down the opposite path towards the colony. She quickened her gait with her shoulders back, and her head held high, smiling even though no one was there to notice. The health of the tree, the produce in her bag, and most of all the company of the young Edward, she hit the jackpot today. As she bustled back along the path, she glanced up into an almost cloudless blue sky. Then the thumping thud of helicopter blades closed in from a distance. Two corporate choppers passed overhead. Ella twisted her head to escape looking directly at them even as their combined shadows rolled over her like a net cast out to sea. She did not want to calculate their purpose. If she believed Riley, they were coming to collect some part of her as some sacrifice to the altar of the longevity for members of the super-rich. For now, she preferred her bubble of denial to Riley's full-on paranoia.

CHAPTER 3

The quirky wrist alarm tune startled her. Riley allowed her eyes to adjust to the light as she lifted just the corner of the tarp. She reached over for her gun and slowly moved the tarp to the side and pulled herself up to a sitting position. For a full second, she commended herself on surviving a solo stop. Then she saw them. Twenty feet farther up the hill, two small figures dressed in camo were moving between boulders on the hill. Without hesitation, she fired a single shot into the air. They scattered in two different directions. Maybe they were poachers who realized she was not worth the fight. If they were IT pirates, she would not have woken up. She pulled out a bandana and wiped her neck and forehead. Better to swallow her stress; this risk was part of the courier life. Probably kids just out scavenging for food for their pack. Opening her pouch, she counted out a half dozen protein bars and tossed them up the embankment.

Next on the agenda - get to the rest area for a water refill, a toilet break and make up the lost time. She shifted over to a kneeling position, braced her hands against the damp earth, and straightened out her legs to do a yoga plow. Absorbing a jolt to her back muscles, she ignored the heavy ache in her calves as she rose to a standing position. She packed away the gun, and then the tarp, reassembled the bike, and guided it down the hill to the highway.

The GPS showed a common rest stop was two miles up the road. It held the promise of multiple charging stations, clean restrooms, massage chairs as well as ample filtered water refills and even a limited dispensary of free approved healthy snacks. Security was tight, and activities monitored. Around her, clusters of small vehicles headed towards the same place. The decent weather drew them like ants to a sweet morsel discarded on the ground. Two sides of the building formed one giant bike rack with free locks. She squeezed into a slot, set a double lock then moved to the line at the outside security counter. After she presented her citizen's badge, they checked that her license to carry a gun synchronized with her renewable fit to carry permit. Once cleared, she slipped the gun back in her vest. She waited in another line to go through a second security check then passed through double-thick glass doors into the main area.

As she entered the hall, the thunderous sound of all the live conversations echoed up to the concrete rafters with voices bouncing in all directions. To have all these people packed into one place was not her idea of an oasis, but there were advantages. Citizens traveled here to the rest stop to congregate in safety. If you got in here, you were not a vagrant, a wanted criminal, or an insurrectionist. You were a citizen even if you had moved a half dozen times, and did not have a real job. You were a citizen if you voted. Riley never saw the same people twice, but it gave her the sense of being at a festival without the music, crafts or greasy food trucks. It was a place for people to mingle and share parts of their lives without relying on the regulated world of social media. Face to face was the real-time that many people craved.

Some completely ignored the Media channels that fed into giant screens on three of the four high walls. Health Watch, Weather Watch, and the Real News channels commanded the room with giant chyrons. Riley tuned her headset for an updated area forecast. The Air Quality Tracker was alive and claiming wellness today. Cleaner blotches of yellow were slowly replacing patches of touchy orange zones. The screens blasted out a steady downpour of information if you tuned in. More experienced visitors knew how to sort it all out and not drown in the sea of images and words.

For Riley, the audience of travelers was the show worth watching. Most ignored the Health channel. The healthy living advice was rote, and it had not done her much good. On the weather wall, the broadcasters were trying to avoid portraying today's fair weather as an anomaly. The thundercloud/AWE symbols covering the coming weekend elicited a long hiss from the crowd. Minus most sporting events, yelling at news and weather commentary had become a game in itself.

Riley wandered along the perimeter of the hall until she spotted an open massage chair. Sensing no immediate competition, she went straight for it. She settled down for a ten-minute respite of the gentle kneading of her back and neck by soft pretend leather. As the chair base pivoted to look at the super widescreen, the Real News channel was ending a segment on current legislative accomplishments. The required chyron scrolled nonstop at the bottom of the screen: and all of this is true... and all of this is true. The "we all need the truth" avatar, WANT appeared and offered a website for those who wanted to question or challenge the program's contents. Riley remembered voting on this meme - a robot-like figure trying to catch 'the truth' in a net.

Her generation had pushed through massive reforms, and yet somehow it came down to this sensible animation. It was not as noble as the original tenet of the truth will set you free. They conceived a new one. In truth, we must trust or perish. Riley liked to think of it as a curocracy or democracy in repair. Constant scrutiny of every news story over twenty years ago sent her out to join the fray. Now she was able to digest most of what she saw on public screens without going through convolutions of her paranoia, making her double-check every story. Truth finding to her had been a well-practiced discipline. The hooting and hollering in this public place was a way for everyone to let off steam. She listened to the cheers go up for a broadcast piece on denied parole for environmental criminals.

Riley nestled her back, neck, and legs to take full advantage of the chair's precise movements. It was a mental treat to watch the court of public opinion in full session holding every statement on the big screen accountable. The waves and bursts of approval and disapproval somehow refreshed her moral compass. Rehashing the past or truth spotting the present was somehow still her blood sport or a continuous Greek play. Now maybe you could hope to avoid the tragedy part at the end.

The noise pumped her up for her self-imposed mission today. Maybe she was a renegade looking for a new cause. She needed to find out more facts and stop working on hearsay. As the rotating wheels of the massage mechanism reached her tender lower back, Riley let out a soft muffled sigh as she squirmed just a bit to avoid too much contact. She followed the wave of the crowd's focus switch over to the other wall. Multi-colored pills and shiny capsules did a choreographed dance across the screen to encourage the use of some newer longevity supplements. For once, it had something resembling original music to go with it. Back then, there were a dozen commercials every ten minutes of programming. The most tricked out were highly visually tuned images of flashy cars moving on clean, spacious highways, luscious liquors served from sculptured bottles and hazy sensuous perfume ads promising more than they could deliver. She had heard of a channel that had nothing but those old ads, ad porn they called it.

Off to her left, Riley heard a young couple arguing about something. She turned away, hoping not to catch enough of the conversation to make any sense of it. Why get involved in anybody else's idea of what is important in their tiny lives. Better to cocoon herself against conversations that were private in this very public space. She swiveled the chair back to the crowd in the canteen, the public noise, the fans in the stands. The upward pressure of the massaging fist continued to soothe her aching muscles, a visceral treat in her low touch world. When the timer buzzed, she dutifully extracted herself as fast as she could and passed the chair on to the next traveler. She shook out her arms and legs out, then picked up her gear bag and moved towards the food dispensary on the far wall. As she stood in front of the wall of little chrome windows with the tags, she stared at the limited selection. She wondered how many of the protein/fruit/nut bars had she eaten in the last decade. The fake raisins and the nubby nutlike bits were always in the same configuration as if they were sending her a message in code. The super sweet smell of whatever held the approved ingredients together was something her stomach had learned to get past.

Riley scanned the benches and around the four corners of the canteen, looking for a place to sit and calculate the next leg of her trip. For now, every space was occupied. She walked the perimeter of the room just skirting small groups. Some of them were in debate mode with a small audience of heads bouncing atop the melee of words while someone tried to win the argument of the day. Others were focused on someone speaking with an air of authority. She slid past all of it close enough to judge if the subject was worthy of her attention. The jumble of voices did not give her what she wanted, an itch to scratch about missing elders.

Heading back outside, she leaned on the bike rack. If she wanted to snoop around the port city for clues, she needed to complete two more deliveries in less than an hour. She geared up, started the electric motor, and rode towards the city limits. Along the edge of the massive overpass, she looked over at the once busy port. She was old enough to have enjoyed the expansive Inner Harbor, dragon boats, and inside malls with tasty treats and souvenirs and idle time with friends. Even with the mix of old and new, the sight was still familiar. With a couple feet of sea rise, the long ramps to the second floors of refurbished buildings made their own kind of sense. The roof of the old red lighthouse jutted out of the gray water, alone and forlorn. She glided past the rebuilt present. The Aquarium still had some specimens breeding in there, for what purpose, she was not sure. The huge stadium was in disrepair, too much to tear down, too expensive to reinvent. Big crowds were not encouraged anyway.

Priority 1 was to get over to the lone cruise ship anchored in the excavated harbor and to get on the ship and into an elevator, get off at a random floor. The high seas had crept into port space as quick-change artists. NDC (National Disease Control) had tackled shipboard diseases, but the flattening of personal spending economy zapped the travel mode for luxury cruises. She was looking for the ship that once carried over 5000 passengers to the jewel blue sea of the Caribbean and back. Many of these once showy vessels sat in redrawn harbors. They were now outposts and transitional housing for the out of state weather refugees. As far as she could trace, this ship only left the pier a few times a year. The locals named it the ghost ship appearing and departing without a planned schedule.

The first drop-off went smoothly. The old warehouse had been equipped with full scanning equipment, and the guards were used to her. No small talk just here you go. The next one was a new customer, and she endured the pat down and a half-dozen questions about the transaction. To her surprise, they handed her another pouch for delivery. She looked at the label, grateful to see a location directly on her way back. No sweat, she could hedge more time. The bike coasted around the corner of the huge warehouse and across the bumpy dock. Her head reared backward. The hull of the ship was still majestic even with blotches of gray metal exposed under the original white veneer. Sitting in its usual berth, it had the independent power to feed and shelter thousands. Riley stopped and settled back on her seat to take in the whole expanse of the ship. There was uniformed staff on one of the decks. The continuous rows and layers of tiny patios were empty of any sign of personal belongings, even deck chairs. She noted the date and time in her cell as she had only seen the ship at this dock three times in the last year. Despite researching the manifest of the entire local shipping companies, her logistics programs failed to match any detailed information about destinations or cargo or passengers. This was either some high-level private venture or secret government business.

She pulled out a fake delivery label and slid it in the front pocket of one of her empty pouches. The courier bike and uniform would get her through an initial screening. Past the first checkpoint with just a nod and a wave to the guard, she left her bike at the bottom of the ramp almost forgetting to lock it. Throwing back her shoulders, she started up the ramp with an air of - I belong here. She waved the voucher in front of the security guard and tried to keep moving. He stepped in front of her, a solid wall of purpose.

"Nothing expected today."

The bulky man in the unmarked uniform eyed her up and down. With a grunt, he raised his hand.

"I think you want the main office down the wharf," as he pointed off into the distance.

Riley looked at her pouch, absentmindedly, "Sorry, I guess I got this wrong."

She turned to go back down the ramp, trying to hide her defeat. It was too risky to push this ruse further. So much for seeing what was going on this ship of souls. Back at the base of the ramp, she unlocked her bike and followed along the line of the ship towards the other end of the pier. Parked side by side near the cargo entrance were several white windowless Mercedes vans. Despite the daylight, they all had their high beams on. The back of each of the vans was facing the other way, lined up side by side in front of the long tented enclosure that leads up another ramp into the ship.

She sat on her bike and waited. Then she caught a glimpse of someone strapped down on a gurney moving through the long tented enclosure. An orderly type person was at the front, pulling it up the ramp into the ship. Riley positioned herself to look directly through a larger opening in between the loose billowing flaps of the walkway. A flash of silver hair went by as the gurney moved out of sight. A large colorful metallic suitcase was attached and rolling along behind. Soon there was the sound of other van doors opening and closing. Another gurney appeared from behind another van, then another. No IV poles or uniformed medical people, only still bodies being hustled along. Escort after escort followed the same path and the ship swallowed them up one by one.

Riley went for her cell but spied a guard moving quickly towards her. Her foot caught under the pedal for a brief second, making her almost stumble off the bike. She hit the gear and pumped herself out of there. Her head buzzed. Is this what she was looking for? These older passengers certainly were not stowaways. She put what she had seen on rewind in her head. The combination of the restrained bodies and the cheerful travel bags did not make sense to her. How do you pack for oblivion?

CHAPTER 4

A mix of socialists' type slogans and posters shared the limited wall space above Alvi's study desk. Three Blade Runner movies and bumper stickers for personal vehicles no one owned anymore, a One Love poster of Bob Marley and a fighting pose from Bruce Lee all stared down at her as if to ratify her fierce attitude. She poured the murky herbal tea into her mug, set it to the side, and put her hands on the ergo keyboard. Concentration on schoolwork was both a ritual and an escape. She thought about her older sister, Maya who had earned deep cred as a full-fledged journalist with awards and national recognition. Her sister's accomplishments always pushed her to work harder and want more. In front of her was the task of another short thesis for her Ecology VI class. It required a heavy lift with the need for precise sourcing and documentation glaring back at her. Growing up during the ultimate civics lessons live and in partisan rancor made her a discerning researcher. Alvi remembered her classmates becoming persistent skeptics even before they left elementary school. The school staff did not discourage spontaneous speeches in the lunchroom. One day, her sister Maya held court for 20 minutes on freedom of speech and finding the truth. Gut checking anything you read on the internet or the media screen was the kiddie pool of their youth.

By high school, their generation was acting like investigative journalists ready to spread the truth or become hardened agnostics, thinking nothing made a difference. Alvi looked at all her other assignments, the history one she resented. She remembered her parents watching hours and hours of news but shielding her and her sister. Now every new age child over the age of six learned the climate impact lessons along with how government constructed rules to ensure freedom and security. Once dipped in purer waters, there was no turning back. She learned about totalitarianism through metaphors in children's books and movies.

They had to find new heroes. If past generations of children read about wizards, her generation watched live trials of good versus evil. By age 12, she was quoting Benjamin Barber, that democracy was the aristocracy of everyone. In Sex-Ed class, she learned that making babies was hard work. Both men and women had to take pills/injections to be fertile, and then the potential mother another pill for 30 days to sustain the pregnancy past its most vulnerable time. It took a combination of science, luck, and careful monitoring with willing participants to make a new human being. Nothing could be forced, only fostered with motivation and supplements.

Her teachers portrayed parenting as a desirable choice you could have along with a full career and guaranteed government supports. The rewards for not letting humanity die off were lavish by new standards. Couples or single females could have a house of their own along with reliable childcare and maintenance help. She already knew her fertility timeline to the month and year.

She stared up at the old poster of a serene, beautiful mountain trail that occupied a lone corner of her wall. It gave a fake 3D feel of a window to a real place. She thought about what it would be like to travel in a vehicle cross-country, someday maybe. For now, you had to accept a digital representation. She keyed up music from her vault of digital files. Almost immediately, she turned it back down. Her parent's ID tone was playing on her cell. She grabbed it on the second ring.

"Mom, Dad, hi, is everything okay?"

"No worries, no worries."

She relaxed, hearing the calm in her mother's voice.

"We wanted to let you know we are traveling to New Florida in a couple of weeks to see your Aunt Lena. There are extra smart trains going down that weekend. Not sure about the cell service there, but we will let you know."

Alvi leaned forward on the desk, pulled out a strand of her hair and started to twirl it around her fingers. She balanced on the edge of her desk chair and shifted side-to-side, listening, and not listening at the same time. An old feeling came back to her of being small and pushed back into her room to play while everyone else was being super serious about the ugly stuff that was out there.

They chatted about her schoolwork, and her dad asked about her elder charges as he called them. Alvi knew they were talking in protective parent speak as she called it. The conversation continued about her aunt's health until she squeezed out an admission. Going to new Florida was not a casual thousand-mile trip; her aunt was not doing well. Her parents were both upending their jobs for a couple of weeks and making what many still considered a risky trip. There were still too many slivers of broken off humanity out there, small packs of those who did not want government but were ready to scavenge what they could from isolated travelers.

"Promise me. You will stay in touch." Alvi tried to extract a promise from the parents who never let her get away without one.

"We will do as best we can," is all she heard.

She got up from the desk. For a moment, she restrained herself from kicking something or throwing her books to the floor. She put her arms up and then out and stretched down to the floor. Her yoga routine would not work today; she wanted to plow every bad thought out of her way, not take the patience to discipline her muscles. On the floor, she crossed her legs, sat, and tried to meditate. Closing her eyes brought on bad visions, so she looked back up at the posters on the wall. She focused on the word LOVE and brought back a fond memory of her aunt. When she came to visit over the years, she brought little porcelain figurines for her and Maya. They were silly little cherub-like children with wide blue eyes and pastel patched outfits. Alvi never understood their vacant innocent looks like the world was just a big playground where everyone got along. Maybe Aunt Lena was trying to chase away the bullies in the schoolyard with these mini totems. Each time she had sat with the girls and told them a story of being yourself and not letting others define you.

She got up, went to the closet, and got out the box. Only two remained. All the other keepsakes, she had sold for an inflated price. She was always the practical one. You can't buy confidence or re-assurance. Holding the tiny figures in her hands made her realize that her aunt had been trying to pass on her natural optimism to a moody child. Lena had said, "Remember, you can always doubt others, but do not doubt yourself."

The mixed sense of reassurance and uneasiness in her mother's voice at the end of the call was hard for her to shake off. Almost every season was hurricane-prone; one-third of Florida sat underwater. Few people heeded the sea rise twenty years ago as the ocean water pushed up through the manhole covers in Miami. The Keys and their idyllic beauty were long gone. Through friends, she had heard strange rumors about survival lifestyles down there. The big infrastructure tech firms built new flip-up sea walls like those in the Netherlands. Life went on but hurricanes and a high heat season disrupted everything almost on schedule.

Her aunt had lived and worked in the central part of the state in a vast retirement community since coming to America many years before. Alvi knew this was a serious turn for her aunt. In her head, she calculated the longevity text- book response. Her aunt's quotient should be at least fifteen plus more years. It was too obvi- ous to put the red flags aside. She would ignore them for now or phone her parents back and call them liars. Her mother's reassurances had not worked on her since she was ten years old. She switched gears and went to the comfort of positive things. Her parents were capable peo- ple. They had traveled a lot more in their life- times than most. Moreover, she could not stop them anyway.

She felt calmer but only for a moment. Ra- tional thought was her drug of choice, but it had a minimal effect right now. Tears started to cloud her vision. They must be lying to her again. That meant anything and everything could be wrong, but their sense of protect- ing her reigned over telling the truth. When- ever she slipped back from the intense per- son they had helped nurture, she became the coddled baby left scared and alone. She put the figurines back in their box and rose to her feet and kicked the side of the chair but only half-heartedly. With a good breath in then out, she sat down again and swiped the screen and went back to highlighting parts of her reading for her thesis of the week. Somehow, it was more comforting to dive into theories on how to reclaim land and make it viable for sustaining crops and population growth than to think about her parents on a train down through the new East coast.

CHAPTER 5

Ella rolled over, propped her head up, and gazed through the narrow slice of the window at the top of the far wall. The weather app confirmed a distinct moody morning with doldrums to come. A bumpy forecast required a somber tone. "Dress for variable weather, be prepared for sudden changes." Ella knew this meant severe thunderstorms and severe winds or just a few innocent showers. She swung the weight of her legs over the side of the bed, sat upright, and stretched her arms up and out. A day like this did not deserve bouncing out of bed. She slipped on a soft old t-shirt and faded jeans. In the bath area, she turned on the tap, pumped the heating coil, and waited for the water to flow hot. Pressing the washcloth against all of her face at once, she heaved a sigh. Again, she repeated the soothing comfort. In an earlier time, she would have applied moisturizer and a little makeup. This face with all its lines and imperfections was hers and hers alone.

Somehow, the soft creases in her face didn't match the rest of her body; wiry and strong. Her eyes always gave it away. Today's variation of green mixed with gray peered back at her in the mirror. Most mornings, she made herself smile back into the mirror, a kind of wake-up call to meet the day. Today she did not even try to force it. A quick brush through her hair, a hot cup of tea and a breakfast bar, and she slid over to her desk area. When she first moved to work at home, she congratulated herself on such an effortless commute. Now she only had to go a few feet from the bedroom to her den. Today would be haunting and too quiet except for possible storms. She needed distractions to help chase away her nagging inner voice still ruminating on Riley's radar about missing or exploited elders. She could not dispute that a few years ago, there were so many visible older citizens out there, everywhere. Gray heads, silver heads no matter how agile they were. Riley was now claiming that if their faces were on old style milk cartons, they would fill a stadium. Today she yearned to be around real people, not imaginary dead or disposed ones.

A dozen assignments stacked up in her work email. She had transitioned from coding training modules for corporations to making happy noises on the computer with visual art and wise words. They used to call them e-cards, banal but sweet greetings that people sent when it was too late to send a card in the mail. Any time she sat down to use her brain was prime time. The pulp paper shortage made artsy cards impossible to produce. She kept a few relics in an old shoebox on top of even older printed photos. On a gloomy day like today, she was tempted to ignore the present, visit the past, and meet old friends once again by letting her fingertips brush over the bits of color and the texture. Words of condolence, greetings of congratulations meant more in familiar handwriting.

Her designs for digital images and scenarios created pleasantries between people. She did not do perfunctory birthdays and anniversaries - just thought-provoking messages. It took her a minimum of effort to finish the first few orders. Match each request with some simple warm wishes and stir with a tint of optimism. For the encouragement selection, she coded an animation of fuzzy puzzle pieces falling apart then back together for a perfect fit.

"When you think things are falling apart, maybe it is only the pieces of your life falling into place." She hit the key multiple times to watch the pieces fall apart then magically back together again. It was a visual trick with a visceral comfort to it. She sent the draft file off to her production manager and pushed back from her chair — break time.

Leaning against the patio window, she looked up and down and across at the closed shades of her neighbor's windows. Riley's unit sat beneath hers, but today she was at her desk job. No outside time today, even on the patio as the hail started to bombard the building. The uneven rhythm of thump and thud was like being inside a tin can pelted with stones. Ella moved over to the treadmill and stood beside it. She punched up a short audio course, followed by a music track. A brisk 40-minutes of fast walking and listening always provided an antidote to clear her head. A Media report preempted the start of her screen choices. The talking heads were explaining about another upcoming voting referendum. She pushed to record for later authenticated viewing. Voting on any special issue required a minimum of time spent watching news coverage of both opposing sides and an ok score on a simple pop quiz for more complicated matters. Voting was part of your citizen duties. It reminded Ella she had signed up to work two different voter registration days in the coming month.

You had to vote to be on the rosters for Universal Basic Income and other goods and services. Public service announcements about building a strong democracy and protecting the rule of the law were not as frequent now. Almost everyone showed up on Election Day. Ella could only imagine what they were teaching in school civics classes. They were truth finders, truth-tellers these young ones. Why did she have to struggle? The young ones would not stand for Riley's wild theories. They would demand proof. After a short infomercial about preventing lizard brain, Ella switched to an old favorite on the National Parks. Her pulse was steady, and her pace quickened. Her loose sentiments were settling down as she watched the vistas of mountain ranges and the unspoiled Arctic. At the end of her time, she stepped to the side of the machine. The app registered her progress, and her stats as always were way above average. Riley had been telling her this would be her downfall, that she was waving a flag, saying look at me I am an outlier come and get me I am research worthy. She had even suggested that it would be better to disconnect the link to the Institute or mess with her stats.

Her work phone pinged more incoming emails. Back at the desk, she scrolled down and saw another special delivery message from the Longevity Institute. This time she stopped to read the complete subject line...a unique invitation to participate. Her mouth went dry, and she put her head in her hands. Looking back up, she glared at the message and moved it unopened to her Institute folder. Her escape path was to go back to her work orders and attempt to push some of her new energy into making more greetings. Then she heard a seldom-heard sound from her unit intercom. It was Alvi.

"Ella, you have visitors down here asking to come up, they look official... may I allow them access?"

CHAPTER 6

Riley got to work on time and slid into her cubicle. She had forgotten again to listen to the weather watch channel but missed the start of the downpour. The hail started its random drumming against the wide windows. Hunger noises rumbled up from her stomach. In her rush not to be late again, she'd passed on breakfast. There would be something to nibble on in the break room. She booted up her unit and logged into the travel logistics of the courier company. Her dual role as a courier and a logistics planner was a fortunate fit. Her eyes ran down the manifest seeking any future delivery that would take her past the ghost ship or over to the rail yard. Living near both a port and train lines gave her a bold sense she and Ella always had a real escape route. She stressed this to Ella even though she never exactly defined what they were running from. Riley strained to find any trace of a travel order for the type of vans she had seen at the port. With no signage to identify even a transit company, it was a lost cause. Whoever arranged these transfers had their own private system.

Algorithms handled the task of checking delivery requests, routes, and schedules, but the weather patterns could act as the spoiler, challenging all movements all the time. The more analytical part of her brain did its mapping as to why some routes were not practical. In a climate-cloistered society where most went nowhere most of the time, she at least got to play in the traffic that still existed. Riley imputed the new list of requested deliveries, destinations and their level of urgency and set the algorithm to sort. Later she would double check it manually with the weather predictions and tag what she wanted for her own assignments. The courier business flourished, even smaller startup companies thought their information worthy of proprietary treatment. Theft of ideas remained a very profitable crime. New approaches to problems had become the new gold.

This breed of capitalism/socialism had matured even while concentrating on massive survival efforts in food production, sustaining a water supply, and advancing medical and education standards. Full Pharma/Food enjoyed the riches of a captive market but had to pay out dividends in UBI. Everyone still looked for that spark of an idea that would turn back time or paint a more predictable future. Riley stretched out her legs and shook them gently to lessen the stiffness. Too much sitting still — off to the break room, she checked first to be sure her favorite people to avoid were not in the room. Dodging of light conversation contributed to her oddball status. With a little effort, she could be more sociable, but most of her coworkers were ten to twenty years younger. Her gray roots at the base of her fuchsia puffs of hair also set her apart. How did she get to be the oldest one in the office?

Some whined about how things were. Others wanted to relive how life had been before. She wanted neither. Riley had given up even pretending she cared about those conversations. Her original posse of real friends had scattered into different city-states to find their ways of getting by. If she had not met Ella as a Temp at her old company, she would not even have a place of her own, let alone a regular job. Riley surveyed the offerings on the snack counter. She picked up two small 'fruit' bars. You did not miss what you did not know, so most here would not recognize junk food if they saw it. Sometimes she could kill for a bag of salty, crunchy chips.

Two of the younger women grabbed a table in front of her. Riley heard the course of the conversation take a familiar turn. They shared the same fertility doctor and the hope that getting their second pregnancies started would be easier than their first. The chatter was about temperature charts, progesterone supplements, and counting days.

"My husband doesn't complain about the hormone shots. He is not that good with keeping track of days; it is all up to me."

The younger one piped up, "Well if you want children, you have to follow the rules or no baby, but having a sex drive helps."

Both women giggled with their own-shared expectations. Riley had a brief flicker of being in her twenties and worrying about birth control and STDs. Now all of that was upside down.

At the other side of the counter, she heard some of her coworkers talking about a mix of fantasy football and politics. To her back, she heard gossip about a new vacancy. No one in this company ever complained about the job itself. If they fired you in the morning, HR could replace you by noon the next day. There was an ample supply of qualified applicants for office positions. For the rest of her day, she shuffled through a dry routine. She stole some time to join some of her old chat rooms looking for more evidence of older citizens just disappearing without a trace. All the statistics on population were on the newest generation being brought painstakingly into the world. It was as if no one cared about those closer to leaving it.

She swiveled, rocked her expensive office ergo chair, and fought her usual mounting claustrophobia as the afternoon waned on with no more excuses to get up and move. She needed a force field to keep her in this cubicle. Maybe one more reason. She went down the hall, up the stairs to double-check the giant whiteboard with any last-minute changes. Her fidgeting brought too much attention, and she knew her office nickname — Restless Riley. There was another ergo-friendly group stretch break at 3 PM, but it was not enough. The days in the office were marginally tolerable. She would schedule herself on the road every single day if the weather allowed. A steady job was a prize, but now she admitted to feeling trapped. At night, her dreams mirrored a mouse that never stopped moving to break out of a maze. As she got ready to leave for the day, she checked her phone. The ringer had been off. She had missed three urgent texts from Ella.

CHAPTER 7

Harold took a few seconds to recognize the ring tone from his C3 (Constant Cylinder Companion). The cheery melody belonged to grandnephew Colin. One hand balanced on his cane. The other swung over to poke the remote button on his wristband. He made his way over to his desk and lowered himself with care on to the counter stool. Leaning forward, he waited while the screen produced an image. Contact with his honorary grandson was not something he took for granted. He recognized that Colin's interventions were the reason he had more time to stay in the colony. His brother's grandson was in his early thirties, married with two children. Without a family member in regular contact, he would find it impossible to keep up with the standards self-management required. Colin had installed the recumbent bike when the treadmill was too much. He liberated some of Harold's trust savings for the advanced shower system. Like many of

the last of the boomers, Harold retained a final crumbly piece of his financial rock. He did
concede with Colin's push to donate a decent
amount to some common causes every month,
but generosity was far from a natural impulse.
He had been able to insulate himself from the
worst of the shortages and remain physically
comfortable. His brother succumbed a long
time ago to cancer before the cure. Colin even
made an effort to have Harold come to their
tiny house and visit the family. The energy of
the two and four-year-old had almost sent him
into heart palpitations. He thought they were
fascinating to watch, like observing an endan-
gered species. That short visit reminded Harold why he felt fortunate in avoiding fathering
children despite being married three times. He
possessed only a limited amount of patience,
and parenting was exhausting.

The screen cleared, and there was Colin's
sweet face with a measure of toddler noise
in the background. "Hi pops, just checking
in. Are you getting out much? How are those
new meals I sent over?" he fired off in rapid
succession.

"Glad to see you, yes they are much better
than the regular stuff. I almost went out the
other day."

Harold tried to be quick as he could on the comeback. Talking to his spirited grand-nephew was like being on a timer. The conversation moved on to what was new about the kids, and then he dropped the real reason for the call. A third child was now on the way, which meant the family was allowed to apply for a bigger house in a different city-state and take their assigned nanny and housekeeper with them.

"We have to think of schooling, they are almost ready for primary level," Colin said. Harold's stomach did a flip-flop. The option of better geographic relocation and job prioritization was a competitive process for every family. Colin's wife also had a solid career and would have her pick of assignments as well. He drew a curtain in front of his thoughts as he felt his mood slip into a drama of self-pity. Everything would be different if they moved too far away. He felt the effort to smile back and reflect the excitement of the earnest young man in front of him.

As Colin jumped off the call, Harold turned off the screen, moved over to his big comfortable chair and let it swallow him up. As he put his hands to his forehead, he told himself that agitation was not the right response. He anticipated that this day would come - this was the sign. Accepting stepping down to a lower level of existence, a move to a group-supervised situation was not on his to-do list. Without a relative within easy visiting distance, he would become an elder ward and orphan yet he could only depend on staff at the colony for very basic external help. How this kind, young man attached himself emotionally to his hard shell remained a mystery to him. Over a decade ago, the future barely belonged to anyone. Harold came through it all only with his grandnephew's patience and guidance. As he perched back even deeper in the furrows of his chair, the guilty realization pressed in on him. He had been making it all about himself for most of his life. His last words to Colin just now were a surprise.

"Well, well, we certainly have something to celebrate."

In his head, he saw their future as more secure and his less. In his heart, he knew this was how it should be. Harold signed off the visual feed with Colin and sunk slowly back in his chair. For a moment, his arms and legs were not as real as if they had been erased. So this is what it means to fade away. Fighting back, he willed his arms to push against the solid sides of the chair and tried to sit up straighter.

He let his thoughts gather as he waited for the unpleasant feeling to pass. Maybe this was the sign he knew was coming, the event that would force a decision on his part. He had lived his life smug in his own belief that things would always work out for him. The world turned upside down for over a decade, and he held on to most of his savings, his health and most importantly his ability to live by himself. The idea of having to move to another place and losing his cocoon of music and his simple cycle of self-indulgence was not acceptable. He remembered what his parents had gone through, the escalator down from one level of care to the next until they were spoon-fed. Those places had disappeared for the most part but so had most of his old friends and colleagues.

His grandnephew had said some reassuring things just now. The family might move closer as his wife worked for NIH and had a promotion coming up. They might move to the capitol area after the new baby was born. Three children guaranteed a bigger house subsidy and at least one full-time nanny and a housekeeper. On the other hand, he knew that the new Pacific Northwest was still a magnet for the more progressive-leaning parents. Different parts of the country were trying to claim that they could keep you safe and free at the same time.

Even though he had never fathered a child, Harold understood how every decision you made affected their lives. Their move to the northwest would be too far away to help him retain his status here at the colony. Colin mentioned an open invitation to visit, but that was only a nice fantasy. His playlist started on a timer, but he hit the remote in his pocket, no music right now, he needed to let this entire scenario sink in. This feeling of self-pity felt strange and out of place. Surely, he still could get what he wanted.

CHAPTER 8

Riley went up to the main office floor again to double-check her deliveries were all properly recorded for the week with no changes or updates for tomorrow. Her assigned bike stayed in the garage at the company's headquarters as she had another office day tomorrow. Getting home on a bad weather day was always bothersome but doable. The train platform of the commuter line was only a two-block walk from the office. The ride would put her back in the colony in twenty minutes. The rain pelted the walkways, but the hail had stopped. She zipped up every part of her light jacket, realizing again that she had left the eco suit at home. She passed on the pick one/leave one stormbrella at the exit door.

Dinner was on with Ella tonight as planned, but her muddled texts brought a new urgency for a face to face. Hard to decipher, was her friend excited or anxious? Now was the right time to confront her with what she had seen at the port. Going over and over it in her head, she hoped this would convince Ella that all was not as it seemed in this new society where longer life was now possible. For now, she hoped the train ride would be uneventful. Most passengers were silently catching up on their personal devices with the net credits they saved by not using them at work. Rationing was the new normal even for unseen things like connectivity. The world had almost choked on too much in your face, instant communication.

Ella's three texts made sense in a way, but Riley didn't understand the last one. Being somewhat older, Ella had never mastered the art of using letters to be the language that Riley's generation had invented. YOU WILL NOT BELIEVE – in CAPS. That was too open to interpretation. Around her, someone swore about a debunked news story over his or her headphones. For the most part, the commuting passengers just drifted along with their favorite old media, music, and pod talks pulsating in their heads. Riley people watched as usual. On a simple commute like this, she first picked up information about people's older relatives disappearing and their cremated remains just showing up for a memorial. To Riley, the best social medium was listening to others' conversations.

As she exited the train, the line for a covered jitney ride up to the colony was snaking out the other end of the station. Her calf muscles ached from the 50-mile ride the day before. So she waited, she wasn't going to hike the rest of the way and soak through her clothes again as the skies persisted in dumping more rain. Finally, she stepped off the jitney and looked up the hill. The odd shape of their complex always seemed comical and familiar at the same time. She imagined someone had taken several stealth bombers and stacked them on top of each other. With the extra green landscaping courtesy of their young caretaker, the whole complex looked like a strange bird creature trying to build a nest into the side of the hill. When the weather defense shields engaged or the solar flower panels deployed to catch any extra sun, it appeared as if a giant insect was arching its wings on the back of a giant bird.

She unlocked her front door, went right to the corner of the kitchen, and tapped a cleaning wand against the metal sides of the trash/recycle shoot. With her unit directly below Ella's, she could send up a simple signal without wasting text time. It translated to; I am taking a shower to be up in 30 minutes. In the shower, she looked down at her right upper thigh. A dark purple mark was spreading there. Maybe something protruded from the ground on the hillside when she napped by the road. She dressed and stared at her short yet somehow unruly hair. Even wet her pronounced gray roots glared back at her. She would do her henna dye routine, maybe later tonight.

* * *

Upstairs, Ella looked at her watch when Riley signaled her. She pulled out her meager bounty from the farmer's market, the kale leaves and re-constituted dried fruit and nuts. In her head, an old recipe for a Kale Caesar salad with ripened figs with balsamic dressing and warm crusts of ciabatta bread and freshly shaved parmesan cheese popped up. She played it in her most edible memories list, a complicated recipe but a savory combination. Tonight, in grand imitation, she threw alternative ingredients together and got out her ubiquitous ranch dressing. The thin milky white substance tasted like nothing she could remember, but it always helped with the illusion. Then there was the tofu.

Having dinner at least once a week with Riley had become both a positive yet unnerving ritual. She tried to keep the conversation on general topics, but Riley always brought up her theories about a sinister end game for weak or older citizens. Ella knew how to rebuke her logic, yet the bits and pieces of fact versus fiction kept adding to Riley's elder doomsday scenario. Ella ran over her usual comebacks. She had somehow mastered the art of agreeing just enough to avoid aggravating her. It was like arguing with an inquisitive child who always needed one more piece of information. Riley's theories deserved at least a what if. Today she may have faced a piece of the puzzle with the Institute at her front door offering trips and gifts to lure her out of her comfort zone. Now the emails and phone messages made sense, or did they? What citizens viewed on the Media News certified as accurate, but what if they were avoiding this subject?

Who or what did all this research benefit? Public service announcements came and went while new supplements and age-reversing treatments appeared and then were withdrawn. Despite all the deprivations, the new discipline of education, work, and healthy living were elongating the life cycle for those fortunate enough to be on the government rolls. Things had turned from survival to recovery in a world that had lost so much from climate destruction.

Ella heard different rumors about those who were too weak or old to live independently. One theory was that they were migrated to designated facilities then hurried along in death. People could be making stuff up about rational suicide. Published obituaries seemed to be obsolete. There was no longer a census every ten years as the government has the power to count heads, whenever they wanted. The front edge of the age wave of the boomer generation had crested and was crashing against final shores. Ella just wished they would be upfront about it. Riley took the more sinister conspiratorial approach.

She did a slow turn to take in the few hundred square feet that held all the pieces of her former life. Here she had work and respect from the members of the colony. Being alone in a big house the last few years after her husband's death was tough. Maybe just having a decent life was the lower rung on the happiness ladder and it should be enough. Living here was a convenient way to push fear aside. All the necessities of life came to your door. Water and power sources were dependable with onsite maintenance. Outside this protected enclave, sizable parts of the population dealt with trying to find new homes and a predictable life. She survived so much in her life even before the upheaval. Living each day now amounted to a default setting, and maybe that was all she was due.

She was drawn to Riley's quirky personality when she started as a temp contractor at her old company. Ella admitted to herself, Riley filled the role of the younger sister she always wanted but was too old to haunt her as the daughter she never had. They were both wise enough to have the perspective of what had gone before, but could they decide together what to do about the future? Ella wanted security but wanted to explore what was out there. Riley wanted to fight injustice and expose corruption but not risk what she had gained in the new system. They were two walking talking contradictions. Maybe they would banter this forever like a no-win game of tic tac toe. Better to call it a draw than to risk too much.

Riley always knocked and avoided the 'zombie' buzzer. Ella leaned over to remote the front door. Riley made her usual entrance with a passable smile and presented her with the surplus catch of the day.

"Special delivery" she declared in a mock deep voice.

"All the protein you can eat with the taste of decades past."

They both laughed at the new slogans on old things. Then Riley gave her signal for talk later — not now.

Ella sighed. Part of their usual dinner ritual was to hold off on any heavy subject until after they ate. Her bold texts had not elicited a spontaneous response. Ella took the tofu roast, cut it into slices, and placed it in the hot pot. They sat down at the counter to eat their almost Caesar salad. The tofu made its presence known with a marginally appetizing aroma. They bantered about their week.

"I saw the most adorable little one in the park today. He had chubby little arms and cheeks. Children are starting to look less like scarecrows. The nanny was not overprotective, so I had him sitting on my lap!"

Riley complained as always about having to listen to the bland gossip about people at her office. Ella listened with her usual level of politeness. She did not miss the office politics of having to pay at least minimal attention to your work mate's lives. As they finished the meal, they both went to their respective corners, shut down the power on the companion cylinder, powered down the treadmill, and put a dishtowel over the microwave. Privacy had earned a renewed high-value point after all the drama of the last two decades. There was no reason to believe that anyone would randomly plug in and listen to their chatter, but Riley still insisted on this ritual when they discussed 'the future.' As far as anyone knew or cared, they were two peaceful, productive citizens in a well-established climate protected colony in a stable city-state. On opposite ends of the old sofa, they both sank down and faced each other. Ella sensed that Riley was in overdrive, eager to approach her once again with theories. She had barely eaten any dinner, and her mind appeared to be roaming miles away, farther than usual. Ella knew to get out of the gate fast.

"I have to go first this time."

Riley crossed her arms.

"Okay, what showed up at your door today?"

Ella spun her tale of allowing Alvi to buzz in two visitors, opening the door and being greeted by two Institute reps complete with broad smiles and huge nametags.

"They came with a small wagon filled with plants and other goodies. It was like that old thing; you know the prize patrol but no balloons or giant checks. I guess ignoring them made me a challenge. They want me to go to Florida for a special session."

Riley glared at her. "You let them in? You think a research trip to see New Florida is a reward. Don't you realize they could be singling you out for harvesting of something valuable in your genetic makeup?"

"Well, at first I was kind of in shock, but they seemed so positive. They brought some good stuff. I politely listened to their pitch at the door, and then took the plants and the brochure on the trip. They offered to schedule a lawyer to go over all the legal papers. Turns out my emails the last two weeks were all about this invitation."

Ella sensed Riley was ready to jump off her seat and pace, but then she would have to shout, and that was not happening right now. She watched her friend sit on her hands.

"They are asking me to go to the main Institute grounds in Florida for two weeks for more tests and observation. I have achieved some level of uniqueness in seven of the nine points of superior longevity data. The brochure makes it look like an all-expenses-paid vacation where you come out better, and so does medical science. They had testimonials."

"And you fell for that? You can't equate this with a web review of vacation stays! Ella, you cannot risk being totally under their control."

"I gave them a tentative yes. I have to go to my doctor and get it cosigned. They explained I would have a travel chaperone and that conditions have improved on the way down to New Florida. They are calling it a time of growth and renewal. It is something I want to see. I can't spend the rest of my life in these four walls and a 2-mile hike back and forth to the community center. "

"Stop, stop...is the trip by train or ship?"

The look in Riley's eyes startled her.

"The new coast trains, of course, the double-wide one. You have seen it on the news, the train is climate protected and escorted through some of the more volatile areas."

Riley went silent, for once. Ella could tell she was gathering her energy to dissuade her. She braced herself and started thinking up a counter-argument as her friend uncurled from her sitting position and stood at the end of the couch like a panther ready to strike. She turned away quickly, walked a few paces, then came back to the same spot.

"Enough with the prelude tell me what you are thinking."

Riley launched into her story in a hoarsely whispered tone.

"I am still trying to make sense of what I saw yesterday. I tried to get on the ghost ship in the harbor, but a guard waved me off at the last check-in point. As I came back down the ramp, I rode past another entrance and saw what I think were several elderly persons (the gray hair always gives you away) being rolled on gurneys into the back entrance of the ship."

Ella put down the mug she was holding and grabbed the pillows to surround her. She played out the scene in her head and shivered. Then Riley painted in the brushstroke of the luggage.

"There were brightly color pattern suitcases being rolled along attached to the back of the gurneys. You know the tourist type."

"Were the people conscious?" Ella asked.

"I am not sure. It happened so fast, and I could not linger very long, and a guard was moving towards me."

They both looked in each other's direction without making eye contact. Finally, Ella rolled her eyes and tried to laugh, but it came out awkwardly, like a sinister advertisement, "Planning for a ghost ship vacation?"

From that point, Riley launched into a review of her greatest hits of how this supported her theory of corporations culling the elderly population either of the sickest or the strongest. Genetic science and longevity research was trying to build the perfect formula for a long healthy life from the winners and the losers. It would be available only to those who could still pay from their wealth.

"Don't think this cannot happen; think what the wrong people could gain from deceiving the public into thinking this could not happen."

She pushed even deeper into the idea of a plot.

"I believe that a few of the remaining wealthy capitalists have bought out parts of the government-run Institute and are using it for their purposes. For decades, the richest people have cared about two things: amassing wealth and finding a way to live forever to spend it. Doesn't it make sense that those who have the most wealth could buy themselves into a longer life span even at the expense of others?"

Ella now sat on the edge of the couch, ready to get up and run away, but this was her apartment. She felt sour nausea rise to the back of her throat. Her usual push back against the sinister nature of Riley's rants did not work right now. The reality of the incident at the dock jump-started her imagination. Having been associated with the leading edge public Longevity Study for almost 20 years, she understood that picking the winners and losers for longevity was now a state-of-the-art science, but were private efforts turning longevity into a buyers' market?

Riley sat back down and finally looked directly at Ella. "Don't you understand? You have something of superior biological value that they want. What is it going to cost you to make them happy? I am aging faster than I should; we are both at risk here."

Ella shifted farther into the corner of the couch. She closed her eyes and let her head sink slowly into the pillows in front of her. As she drew herself back up, she willed her expression to be a shield against Riley's blind logic while fighting feelings of guilt over her own greediness. She was already living healthier than most people were her age, but wanted to break out of this fortified birdcage.

"How do you know what is going to make me happy?"

Riley went silent, for a moment then blurted out,

"What does happiness got to do with it?"

They both had circled, but they were back at a familiar place. Ella repeated her usual rant on what had gone well in the last few years. "Health care and medical research have somehow held fast and even moved forward through the worst of all environmental challenges. News sources and social media stopped being a battleground of who had more sites to push their truth. Fertility clinics are high tech and free, so people are having children again."

Riley countered again with the fact that for several months, the studies on the longevity achievements have stopped being part of the regular media feed. "Why are they no longer boasting about who lives to 110?"

"Well, maybe those birthday celebrations are tedious," Ella shot back.

Riley repeated her view of the truth as truth.

"Except for old Harold up top, how many advanced aged citizens do you rub elbows with anymore?"

"Okay, so traditional nursing homes no longer exist, and many old retirement communities now house weather transients. How are you supposed to determine what is happening when you cannot get out of your own city-state without a visa? If I had lived somewhere else and come here, maybe I would know more."

As Riley started up again, Ella stopped her.

"You are paranoid about a worst-case scenario. We both have jobs, privacy, and our own money on top of the UBI. We can come and go as much as anyone could with the weather restrictions within certain geographic boundaries. If we don't leave for too long the risk is not that high."

They both sat in silence for a short time. Then Riley kept going, "They are not even running obituaries any more. I have tried to get into the census databases, and they are not open to the public."

Ella countered, "They are curing so many diseases. You can get optimal replacement body parts. Old age isn't what it used to be.

There have to be other reasons why elders disappear. People move back closer to family at the end if they have a family. Just because you drop your social media presence does not mean you don't exist. It's not mandatory."

Riley sat there, and a look of dismissal walked across her face. She was in her winner versus loser mode. Sometimes Ella knew that Riley's best defense was silence as if to say, I had the last word, you can babble on.

Time to change the subject somewhat; Ella went over to her desk, pulled out her tablet. She scrolled through her email. "I got this several days ago, but I didn't want to read it. The Institute people explained the advanced study to me today. I never read the initial invite."

"Open it ..." said Riley, "I want to see it."

Ella scrolled to display the notice. She held it out in front of her like a town crier ready with a proclamation.

After years of participation in our Longevity Study, we are strongly requesting your full cooperation in bringing our study to a new level. We are seeking long-term members like yourself to join us at our leading research headquarters in Lakeland, Florida, for a two-week stay... We will provide travel arrangements, all-expenses paid .... You would be accompanied by a health wellness aide...the goal is the betterment of society and your personal future longevity etc. etc.

"Okay so, is there anything in there about being able to refuse all this?"

Ella hunched her shoulders and turned away. The commanding undertone of the request stoked her growing doubt head-on.

Riley regarded her friend with a mixture of triumph and regret as Ella shrank back on the couch again. All these months of tidbits of information were now piled up with her discovery of the gurneys at the pier. She had finally driven her friend into a mute corner.

Riley let the silence well up around them. She decided to throw out another solution. "Well if you insist on going I can probably cop a coding/courier trip in the same direction. I can be on that same train south, and we can face this together, whatever it means."

Ella looked over at Riley. She was as serious and matter of fact as she always was. That would be two chaperones. She grabbed her remote and flipped to the main media screen to stop the conversation. Riley understood this was the signal not to push it further right now. It was Ella's decision to make.

They switched to a new podcast of an old favorite weekly news commentary program. Many older citizens watched both the old and new segments to remember times of doubt and turmoil over what government was supposed to be and then reflect on the steady progress of now. Like an old movie, you knew the ending, but you wanted to live through the drama again. Their favorite iconic news anchor only broadcasted once a week now but still handled the complexity of the issues with scholarship and humor. The old type of reporting had spawned another generation of journalists on the watch for everyone's freedom and true liberty. They both could continue the debate on what to do about Florida in their heads but welcomed the timeout.

The program signed off with the... and all of this is true... chyron scrolling across the screen. Ella sat in her own emotional fog, and then her anxiety broke through. The interlude of watching the TV compounded the tightness in her chest and the shallowness of her breathing. This time she could not add her positive poker chips, subtract Riley's negatives, and come up with a win – not even a draw. She went back to the sink to start cleaning up. Nothing that Riley brought up tonight could be disregarded.

She kept her back to Riley, hoping she would take the hint and leave. Riley was not always good with social cues, and Ella dreaded spending more time hashing this out. She flinched when Riley came over to her and gave her the briefest of hugs, a big deal for her touch aversion friend. They were no longer at their usual stalemate. Maybe Riley felt her caving in yet somehow realized it was better not to continue to make specific plans. Riley was going to let her wrestle with her conclusion. Was she off to a welcome break from her four walls and the little Colony, or was she playing right into the hands of those who marked her as a biological prize?

Riley excused herself. "I have got a split day in the office with maybe some short trips tomorrow; I better get some extra sleep."

Ella waited to hear the click of the door lock.

CHAPTER 9

Ella scrubbed the plates, staring at each line of the intricate floral border patterns as if they could be read like tea leaves. This was her real china, not the thrice-recycled plasticware you bought now. Holding the heavy plates still reminded her that she had time to pack her most precious things, while others became weather refuges left with the clothes on their backs. Hers was a particular brand of survivor's guilt. Yes, she had been able to sell her place and move into a living space that would not be blown off the ground it was built on. There was an ordered routine to her life while others lived patiently waiting for any predictability.

What she had left behind was a life of watching others succumb to diseases and disasters. She had held people's hands, attended funerals and written long sympathy notes. All the while, her health checks had bolstered her sense that she was coming to live well for a very long time. What was wrong with wanting to tease more out of her bonus years? Riley still existed by her old mantra, do not let the other side lie to you. She was always fighting to be on the winning side even when there was no longer a manifest enemy. Sometimes you have to go along for the ride. She put the dishes in the drying rack and shifted back over to the couch.

She retreated into the indentation of the old suede upholstery and stared blankly at her bland walls as the sadder spirits of her mind came back to berate her. She could not fluff it off. Was there a logical explanation for what Riley saw at the port? Maybe they were being transported for medical treatment. So much for the shadowy absence of older elders, this was very concrete, hustling old folks off for what could be an involuntary trip. She had fought a slow creeping suspicion for more than two years. Others in her generation had participated in long-term surveys and health scans. In the beginning, it was kind of a lark, 'seriously seeking centenarians' was the slogan for one popular campaign. Now she had lost track of so many old acquaintances and friends. Emails were never answered. Cell numbers were defunct.

Except for the years she struggled with infertility, Ella always enjoyed good health. She was fastidious about diet and exercise long before it became an expectation. Having lost contact after the funerals was nobody's fault but her own. Social media grid was not the penetrating force it once was, and that was overall a good thing. Lives changed and re-established themselves. It was as if everyone had temporary amnesia for a period, and many were willing to forget the worst of it. Several friends, a bit older, had just disappeared. Did they all succumb to the only incurable type of dementia? All this clashing of views was starting to peel away her usual layers of simple it has to get better optimism. She did not want to live out her life in the colony and be grateful for what she had. It was okay to want more than this cocooned life. At least she wanted to see what was out there. The risks were starting to stack up like bad Tarot cards. There was the exploitation then discarded card from the Institute. There was the kidnapped by road pirates scenario. Of course, there was the death count card from a variety of weather events.

She ran her fingers over the pattern on the couch pillow, tracing the intertwining concentric circles repeatedly. Where did she fit in the sphere of life, or was she confined in a cage? At a time when others were spiraling down to less, she wanted to reach out for more. Maybe these were just more gray thoughts at the end of a gray day. The weight of her mood pressed her even tighter into the corner of the couch until there was nowhere else to move. She pulled the fleece throw around her shoulders and curled up inside her brooding cave. Her thoughts went back to the night her husband did not come back from an errand. They had argued and he went out to escape her dark mood. The next thing she knew, she was identifying a body at the morgue. He was the victim of a single random gunshot. She was the survivor, but for what? Was it her fault or just fate? They had grown apart even in their marriage. She had felt tied down and restricted by duty. Then he was gone. The self-pity tasted sour on her tongue and lips. Bitterness was never a friend, only an enemy that can destroy what is left.

She stared at the picture of her sister's only child. In the fragile Popsicle frame, she saw all the promise and vibrancy only pre-pubescent girls could muster. Her smile was confident and her eyes were penetrating. Remembering all the time spent with her, the gifts lovingly selected and appreciated was always a brief respite before the fearless image turned shadowy. Her niece dead before she turned twenty-five. Always and again the question, why she couldn't help when it really mattered. It can't all be fate. She wanted to kick that excuse to the curb. Right now, the weight of her head on her knees and the warmth of her arms wrapped around her legs was her only comfort, and the only thing that was real. Slowly she inhaled the warm air, held it then let the sobs explode from her lungs. She remained that way until she felt the dampness of her tears on her knees.

At that moment, she wanted the strength to push past old grief and admit she wanted a better future. She was supposed to live in a time when truth was truth. If this was a sinister operation, there was no concrete way to deny Riley's theory. Brushing off the study could have consequences of its own. She would take this chance and go on the Institute trip. Maybe these were gamblers odds, but she felt like she would be the winner and walk away with her version of the prize. The purple lights over the plants by the patio window were dark now. She stirred out of her cocoon to the bathroom; put a warm washcloth on her face, and looked at her eyes in the mirror. The question no longer there, she had the answer.

On the practical side, Riley had pledged to try to schedule a trip to coincide with her Institute dates. There was comfort that Riley wanted to be there with her, somehow protect her from the corporate demons or mad scientists.

It was time to put the whole process in gear, time to stare at the future, and have the guts to act on it. She leaned over to her tablet, initialed several clauses, and replied yes to the Florida research trip. A momentary sense of peace fluttered around her. This was her decision for now. Riley promised to come up with an escape plan if things turned sour. Starting over for both of them was crazy but possible. She knew Riley was the real adventurer, and she did not want to be left behind.

She followed the last of the entire automatic shutdown sequence as it played out in the unit, quasi commands to turn off her brain.

Tonight, she would not sleep as the excitement of making this decision tossed and turned her in the night. Her tiny bedroom was just a dozen steps away, but Ella grabbed another pillow and curled up on the familiar curves of the old couch. She was not going anywhere for now.

* * *

L.I.F.E. Database Control Center - 4.28.2039 – 5:37 AM EST
Location Climate Colony #42
Subject: Ella D 540 752-O

Change in algorithms keys a check/respond alert: Send message: Bio-Genome Harvest Project: Priority 1 B status

Tech One: Life Bit registers only 30 minutes of sleep in last 8-hour period. All other vitals normal.

Tech Two: No need to intervene. She has accepted our offer and will be coming this way. That is worth losing a night's sleep. As Shakespeare wrote, *sleep perchance to dream of a future to unfold.*

CHAPTER 10

Once back in her unit, Riley looked at the supply shelf and grabbed the right chemicals from her last Big Pharma/Food order. She applied the hair dye. Towel around her head, she lowered herself into her most comfortable chair and watched more news media while the color set. This time she added a mix of purple with rose tints for the tips. She enjoyed the curious looks when she changed it up. In the long humid summers, she did not bother to cover most of her old tattoos. Their original blazes of inked glory were once standouts on her forearm and the back of her neck. Now the inked artwork has faded on the canvas of her fifty-something flesh. Anything that set her apart from the norm was ok with her. The tattoos and the hair shouted a message, leave me alone, or accept me for who I am. She had noticed that the kids at the end of the next generation did not bother with branding themselves with inked artwork or piercings. They were marked by their status of being for a while the last of the young.

For the most part, they had been nurtured into the world from childhood to believe that they were both unique and entitled. What was there to rebel against?

At her desk the next morning, she reviewed the roster again for chances to explore around her delivery areas. Ella's letter had three possible dates in the next month to leave for the Florida Institute. Her coding partner Laney shared last week that they could be looking at some more significant assignments even beyond Florida. Riley searched through upcoming deliveries and potential customers and brooded over getting another look at the dock. Nothing came up even near the ghost ship. The possibility of using a drone to reveal more of the activity on the ship had crossed her mind, but major restrictions in privacy preservation laws did not allow remote private camera function. Even if she could manage a quick flyover, they were not that reliable even in decent weather and used only for light loads of unclassified material. The ship sailed the day after she tried to bluff her way up the ramp. She had no idea when it would dock back in the port. She had missed her chance. How would she figure out how many people got on and who came back?

The only other person she had brought up her 'theory' to was Lindy. That was months ago, and her response had Riley back off for a while.

"You have such a dark grip on a no reality. Stop making up an answer to a puzzle that does not exist. Older people die, people perish. Does it mean that some government or corporate entity was sending more infirm or older citizens out of the country?"

Lindy had tried to counter with the logic of places to go for rest and recuperation or a kind of long-term rehab. Riley held to her grim version that maybe the government resettled the most fragile then disposed of them. The conversation had ended with Lindy advising her to get some help for her paranoid thinking.

"Life is tough enough without you making stuff up."

Riley sunk back into her thought bubble. After all the intense research into longevity and vitality, what had they learned? Between the challenges of natural procreation and rigors of dealing with a harsh climate, life demanded to be nurtured at every turn. On the other hand, was there just some kind of cutoff switch out there for those who have had their share of life?

Riley knew her body had the aches and stiffness that even older citizens avoided with supplements. She saw her physical capacity sliding down a scale. She dreaded talking to her doctor about her episodes of weakness. The low-grade fevers and the nagging fatigue kept coming back with no set pattern. She didn't want to become an outlier guinea pig, like Ella. Trust was never a strong word in her vocabulary.

A message popped up for an instant team meeting. She grabbed her tablet and joined the group of her coworkers moving towards the conference room. This was unscheduled; something was up.

CHAPTER 11

When the gray morning light crept into her unit, Ella faced her tablet to confirm her schedule for a busy outside day. The weather app warned of another mixed wonder of fluctuating temperatures and substantial precipitation but no grounding message. She dressed quickly and ate a simple breakfast. First, on her list, she had volunteer time with voter registration for the current referendum and later a regular checkup with the local Institute clinic. The to-do list was a welcome structure even after a night with little sleep. Helping with the voting process was the only volunteer activity allowed. Anything else had to be paid UBI work. The new rock-solid system resulted from all the past scandals of trying to purge voters years ago and was a worthy cause in her mind. Bio scan tech has taken the wind out of the sails of voter suppression. Citizens had to register and vote at least once a year to receive UBI and healthcare. Participation peaked in the 87% range after the Voter's Voice Amendment.

She pulled out her full eco suit and donned it piece by piece. If a climate skirmish broke out today, better be prepared. To save time she grabbed a jitney over to the Colony Center. Working at the check-in desk and having contact with people, not just imputing web votes off in a corner was her preference. The difference between an Arkansas and an Alabama accent stood out to her as she overheard their tales. She spent the morning verifying identities and former addresses. The addresses themselves read like a roll call map of people's fractured lives. How did people end up so far away from their original homes? The reassignment system was not that complicated. People were moving towards other shreds of family trying to knit together a new version of their old selves.

Most people had their previous registrations with them or enough ID to bring them up in the general database. A calm, positive tone prevailed even as they stood in long lines in thrift store hand me down clothes. Ella was eager to reassure them of the rights and privileges, it gave her a soothing sense of putting society back together one family at a time. Ella leaned over and scanned the room to see if any children were scattered among the voters. Only a few had come with their parents even though a voting day was a full holiday from school and work. No elders either. The whole process was going smoothly, with no arguments, maybe just a few muted remarks in front of her. Most people stood in almost revered silence, as they understood this opportunity meant the difference between order and chaos.

The woman stood in front of her wearing clothes that were so mismatched as to be comical. Behind her were three children. The oldest child was holding the youngest one on her hip and giving the middle one orders. As they moved forward in the line progressed, they were never more than two feet apart from each other. Ella recognized the look of accomplishment in the woman's eyes as she laid all the necessary documents on the counter. There were birth and death certificates, an old deed; more paperwork than she needed to register to vote.

Ella completed her part of the process, trying to send back enough of a smile to reassure the woman that she could relax a bit. She handed the woman the standard printouts on health benefits, finding work, UBI deposit schedule.

Next, a bone-thin young man stepped up to her counter. He had that look, of being weary but strong, as if he had been through the wringer and come out just starchy enough to handle life.

"Ma'am, I only have my work papers from my last job, not been here that long, still living in temp housing." He hesitated as if waiting for rejection then pulled out a tattered picture employee ID. "Doesn't look much like me but I swear it's me." Ella looked up at the scruffy soul in front of her and then down at the kinder side of this man's history. The same sincere smile stood out.

"No problem sir, here is your ballot. Follow the other line over there." He relaxed his shoulders, smiled broadly and hustled over to the next line. Ella knew that no matter what the story, the state migrants had a chance at a reconstructed future. Finally, on her break, she glanced over the list of questions Riley had emailed her. She hoped to make the most of her medical appointment today and extract some honesty about why she was such an excellent specimen. Expecting honesty was a weakness of hers. Maybe it was better than Riley's intense skepticisms, but distrust was finally sticking to her.

At first, this once a year review of her mental, physical, cognitive, and social stamina was encouraging. She always left the session feeling validated in her good habits and enjoying the attention of the doctor. Then they moved her up to a twice a year schedule, and now more than one doctor/tech always attended her exams four times a year. These 'visits' were supposed to be for the older citizens to ask questions about any health problems or introduce new resources to help promote longer healthier life spans. At her last visit, they took more samples of blood and even requested an invasive bone marrow sample and other tissue samples that she refused. Keeping a positive attitude was difficult when she felt like she was under a microscope and an advanced one at that. There was always the backdrop of Riley's reverse theory that instead of using the blood of younger subjects to keep people from growing old, they would synthesize anti-aging properties from the not getting old so fast elders.

As she signed out, the next volunteer stepped right in to keep the lines moving. She felt the sweat creep up on the back of her neck as she headed over across the courtyard to the med center. Being confined in her eco suit, an eerie sense of helplessness was engulfing her. She felt that at any second someone could yank her string like a giant puppet and take her off the stage. The rain and the wind seemed incidental; her negative thoughts were out running her calmer core. She spotted a bench and managed to get over to it. Her knees were mushy, her mouth parched. A few sips of water from her travel bottle and she perked back up. She felt invisible, even in this public area. She would either sign the next set of papers or not. This is not how she wanted to walk into the exam, feeling like an emotional ghost.

After last night's conversation with Riley about rolling the elderly passengers onto the ship, she had a half-awake dream. She was deep in the ship's hold and feeling suffocated by heavy blankets. Riley came to save her, and they jumped into the sea. It was not a good ending. She pulled herself up, threw her head back, and made a promise to herself. She would make her own decisions. No one had the right to run her life. As she pressed forward against the wind and the pelting rain, she saw the shining curved surface of the side of the Medical building ahead. It looked like the hull of an ocean ship.

CHAPTER 12

Riley slipped into the conference room and looked for a seat in the back. She was tired of the rote business speak about producing and taking on new challenges. Maybe this meeting would actually be useful for her own purposes. She placed her tablet on the next chair and waved over her coding partner. Lindy had entered the room with her earbuds in place and slouched down on the hard chair.

"What a rip, I was supposed to get that assignment in New Florida, but now everything is up in the air."

A good ten years younger than Riley, Lindy was a solid work partner. As one of the moms with benefits at the company, this office-bound job and her two kids entering middle school were her life. Extra temp nannies took over for her rare trips out of state.

Their director kicked off the meeting with a lame joke about coding then launched into a mild tirade about how he expected the company to be receiving more government work. He stood there with his usual power slouch using his hands like an over-caffeinated mime.

"In exchange for more protection in our cyber updates, we will be doing some of the legwork ourselves." He made a point and waved to the back of the auditorium. "What does that mean for our trustworthy band of super coders? It means that some of you will be working on-site to make these changes."

He asked volunteers to go on a trip to Denmark, to New Florida, and to Shasta Cal; by rail to Florida and California and by boat or air transport to Denmark. He prattled on for a while about how these trips were a priority if the company was to land a bigger share of the IT security market.

Riley heard the rumblings from the other techs, "I am not going anywhere near northern Cal, the Caucasian Nationalist Nation is still there.

"Yeah, I heard they do not stay in their own set perimeter and still like to mix it up."

"They add and lose people but stay self-contained. It's a dead zone to media anymore."

No one wanted any part of that trip. The media rarely covered Shasta except to keep count of the shrinking population. Like the

Shakers centuries before, they would die out of their exclusionist philosophy. No tech, no kids. Their population was spiraling down.

Lindy quipped to Riley, "Too bad Shasta is so close the giant tech campuses, thanks but no thanks."

Riley and Lindy shot up their hands to volunteer for the list for Denmark and/or Florida. They both had a good chance to be selected for both preferred workgroups, as their skills were very generalized and specific in the new codes. To Riley, traveling would be a widening of the circle with more places to look for confirmation of her vanishing elder theories. It would be hard to mount a resistance to stop a practice she could not prove was happening. If elders were being moved around and disposed of, the farther away she was from the tight inner bubble of her city-state, the better for information gathering. She needed something concrete she could take to the news media. Something that could appear in a chyron Breaking News – New Florida is really, where old people go to die before their time.

A train ride to Florida followed by a flight to Denmark could give her exposure to more first-hand information. By the end of the meeting, they had hashed out a tentative team list and she and Lindy stood second on the list for

Florida and third for Denmark. The company needed to schedule the travel soon before the press of the summer heat made life more difficult.

Three hours later, back on the work floor, Riley looked up from her desk. Lindy stood there with a sour expression.

"We got them both, but the New Florida and the follow up to Denmark are all one long trip. I know you are thrilled, but I do not want to be away that long. Someone else will have to do the second leg with you. Twenty-five days is too long to be away from my girls, even with the nanny."

Riley half listened. The next stage of her plan had real potential to snap into place. The logistics were lining up beautifully with a perfect assignment to Florida on the train then a flight to Denmark, where the quantum supremacy and social norms had evolved way ahead of the rest of the world. Years ago, when the states were coming apart at the seams, one of the escape hatches was Europe. She matched the dates Ella had given her. If things turned rotten with the Institute, this could work. Ella could slide in as her substitute-coding partner. It could mean a new beginning for both of them.

CHAPTER 13

Harold sat against the far wall and watched the storm clouds roll over the hills dragging along the next massive onslaught of rain. The flashes of the lightning erupted alternately ahead of the drum of the thunder blasts. The outburst was stomping closer and would soon engulf the building. It was like sitting under a giant metal cone waiting for someone to bang against the sides, lift it and dump water on you.

He hurried to warm up his dinner then turn on his emergency light as a precaution. If the power went out, the units had backups, but falling in the dark would be a dumbass thing to do. He made himself eat half of the bland square of fortified food and then judicially dumped the remains into the trash compactor with thumbs down gesture. Even in his younger time, he did not care about that next great meal or a new cuisine. Persistence in keeping a meal schedule was a defensive move. Being this thin with no reserves was not working well for him.

Tonight, all he wanted was to watch an old film on the new media player that his grand-nephew had sent. Colin had coached him on People Time as to how easy it would be to operate. You had to speak the name of the program to start it, but with all the outside noise, Harold had to shout to make it work. The soft frailness of his voice surprised him, fading in volume and intensity like an old piece of vinyl. The insistent rain pelted on the roof just above his unit. With a futile gesture, he poked at the buttons and managed to power down the player, forgetting he should say, "Volume up." He would have thrown it across the room, but that was also a lame thing to do. He switched back to his music playlist. On nights like this, he realized others often gathered in someone else's unit to share a meal and conversation. People stopped inviting him years ago when his answer was always no. The brittle balance point of being too late to change was now a matter of too old to care.

The doorbell rang with a flashing signal for good measure. Startled, Harold struggled to his feet, asking himself who would be out on this wicked kind of night. He checked the door guard to see who was there before releasing the lock.

"Peace, all I want is some peace," he muttered under his breath.

His body took some time to balance the stiffness and the weakness in his legs as he went to greet the intruder. As he got to the door, it opened. Before him was the sight of Alvi standing there in a bright green rain poncho and muddy boots. The rain was dripping off her curly bangs on to her nose even though she stood under the roof of the walkway. She waited for some kind of signal from him.

"Goodness - come in, what an awful downpour!"

She took a deep breath and put on a smile and stepped in, pausing on the inside mat to dutifully wipe her feet like a well-trained preschooler. A satchel with instruments and tools hung over her shoulder.

"There have been some abnormalities with the power grid, and I am checking to see that everyone is fully operational."

He watched her as she took temporary possession of his space, checking this and that with her small meters. Harold tried to stand a bit straighter, as not to betray any weakness.

Try to be sociable - what should I say.

Alvi stole glances at him as she proceeded to power points in the unit. "Well, you look as if you are doing well for yourself," Alvi said in a tone as if the patient was not him but his electronics. "By the way, I have some philharmonic virtual reality programs if you like to borrow them. Also, there is an outdoor hologram concert that has a floating date outside in the courtyard next month."

The offer to participate directly in something that would be worth the effort soothed him. "Yes, yes, put me down for that." He fought to add a smile, forgetting almost how and feeling quite silly. Nevertheless, she was scrutinizing him as well as every inch of his unit. He waited until she emerged out of the bathroom and secured the meters back in her bag.

"That is an incredible unit you have in there. You must really enjoy it."

"Indeed I do young lady."

He thanked her and watched as she closed the door. He almost collapsed letting go of the tension in his spine. He had survived the encounter and not ended up as a heap on the floor. Up close, she was not so sinister.

CHAPTER 14

Alvi checked the next three units registering a fault and only had to replace one piece of equipment. All the residents in her building were okay or at least feigning normality despite the violent storm outside. On nights like this, she congratulated herself. People adapt, the structure and placement of these living units helped that happen. To come back from her long weekend to have people stranded, even though the elevator had generator back-up, would not be a good thing. That Harold, he seemed okay even sweet in a vulnerable old man kind of way. She tried to put aside her observation skills. He was a stick figure of a man, but that smile and the old hippie attire had won her over from getting too personal about his eating habits. With all the glorious music that played while she was there maybe, he was not so alone after all.

Back in her studio unit, she put on her noise-canceling headgear and pulled up

Dylan's "Things have Changed." She preferred to watch the DVD and try to make sense of the words. She was too young to know the iconic "The Times They are A-Changin"...years between the words about times being strange. How could it have been bizarre when seasons were predictable, politics something you did not talk about that much? Harold's generation was always singing about being forever young. Her generation was mature before their time.

She listened to music that covered years three times her age span. Sometimes she wondered if her peers would ever create their own music when they had to attend to the business of putting things back in order. Her parents had protected and yet hardened her. With so much malice and injustice, swirling about back then, they wrapped her in a cocoon of tough mental love. She never had the choice to have less responsibility on her slim shoulders. Her youth was not a time for teddy bears and lollipops. Because of the color of their skin, stupid people had intermittently targeted her family. Strangers looked at her gray-blue eyes with dark eyelashes and curly hair and were transfixed, as they could not categorize her. Some people were challenged by her mixed ethnicity. She grew to ignore it. Now her youth alone was her identity badge.

By the time she was seven, her vocabulary had included the word hypocrisy. As a middle schooler, she learned the difference between conservatism and liberalism. In high school, she learned the meaning of motivated social cognition. The partisan turmoil made people take sides or drop out of the conversation altogether. However, the dropouts came back into the fray when voting was again safe, certified, and the pure expression of their civic will. You voted, or you did not receive protection from the climate or the right to claim UBI. Ignorance was neither bliss nor acceptable.

Alvi only relaxed when among her peers. They were not the miracle new birth babies. They had to live through the worse before the better happened. They formed their own type of defense shield moving forward together to a fuzzy future. Equal education came at last, and they were the future environmental scientists and technicians, geneticists, new nutritionists. They would have a place in the work world because they had to fill in the long gaps left by the babies never conceived. They would have to cram knowledge in their heads to become the experts, the thinkers, and the doers of what needed to be done.

Those who dropped out of the reforms, who found all this social responsibility a giant waste

of time were out there as well. They were playing their own game of survivor, taking what
they needed from week to week. Their targets
were the old and the young alike.

She switched over to the next song and
laughed at "Another Brick in the Wall" by Pink
Floyd: something about you don't need an
education?

CHAPTER 15

Ella squirmed around on the examining room table. Trying to concentrate on the Self Help Health message on the small monitor on the wall was useless. Maybe age detecting sensors kept looping the video to the segment about fall prevention. She would rather be thumbing through an old magazine about the secret lives of the rich and famous ...an easy distraction from back then. The strangeness of sitting here, not because she had a medical problem but to defend her good health, never went away. Another completed checklist was on the tiny desk. Yes, she exercised so many times a week; her diet was the best of the plant-based substitutes. She consumed all the recommend longevity supplements. Eight and a half hours sleep a night was her average and she practiced meditation in a reasonable proportion to stress. On her last visit, she sat across from the tech and read the notes upside down on the previous survey. "Cheery/very pleasant elder orphan." She resented being summed up in those words even though he had praised her positive attitude. This was another stalemate. They were determined to find her golden key to skip a decade or two of age decline. She was failing at giving them any clear answers.

A knock at the door then it slid open to reveal a crisp young man in an even starchier white lab coat. "Hello Ms. Dunham, my name is Matthew. I have a few more questions for you." He pulled over a stool and proceeded to ask the same questions she had answered before. Ella wondered if this was like a personality test where they repeated the same questions three different ways to see if you were consistent in your answers. She did not want to sound flippant. Like the time she joked about trading part of her DVD collection for fresh blueberries or a real mango. He did his researcher speak; she answered the same way. He played their greatest hits album of trying to discern some habit, something she ate, and something in her background that made her this marvelous specimen. Then he finally landed on to the real reason for this visit.

"I see you responded to the two-week trip to New Florida for some additional studies. We are of course signing off on this for you." Ella nodded as her prepared questions left her head like so much debris in a windstorm.

"Once you get to New Florida, you will be spending time on a stationary cruise ship with some other people your age before you go over to the Institute in Lakeland."

He babbled on about compensation for her time away from work and taking extra supplements before she left. An icy stab went through her stomach up to her spine and almost out of her mouth. Ella tried not to betray the look of panic that her face wanted to make.

A cruise ship!

An image popped into her head – she and her best luggage strapped to a gurney and off to la-la land with just enough sedative to make the trip bearable. Anger was not a suitable response right now, even with this nonsense about the medical power of attorney being transferred from his office to the Institute. Right now was not time to be having visions. She tried to turn her attention back to the doctor.

"In addition, we are providing a full-time companion for your trip. She is ready to meet you now." Before Ella could even recover from the last two surprises, the exam room door slid open. The woman stood about 5' 3" yet had the carriage of a drill sergeant. She stepped into the room and proceeded around the exam table eyeing Ella like a fresh recruit for boot camp.

"Ella, this is Mattie. She has done this before, and I am sure she will be able to answer any of your questions."

Ella stammered a hello. Her usual composure blown twice over, she drew a blank. There was nothing in the notice about a cruise ship. Her mind went back again to her conversation with Riley. That boat in the local harbor ...to Florida maybe. Older people ...gurneys. Ella struggled to form a coherent sentence,

"Yes, I would like to find out more." Mattie detailed the accommodations on the trip and promised a chance to see some of the ecological renewal along the coast. She repeated her question to the doctor as to what made her such an excellent specimen so worthy of all this attention, was brushed aside again with the reassurance she was in a very elite group and should be proud. It was clear the doctor and Mattie were two salespeople ready to hype up this trip as if she had won the lottery.

Finally, the white coat and Mattie left the exam room. Ella took in deep breaths as if the good air had been sucked out of the small space. Maybe they were outside waiting to see how long it would take her to pass out. The doctor's only giveaway was that she was among a group of subjects who had demonstrated higher longevity quotients without having the usual history of parents with exceptionally long lifespans or the usual specific genome factors.

Ella finished dressing and picked up her transportation voucher on her way out of the lobby. The receptionist handed her another packet of information to take home and sign, telling her something about electronic signatures not being valid for final sign off. All the same clauses, we will, you shall and more to study. She pulled the facemask up on her eco suit as she waited for the vehicle. The irritant index ticked high today.

The solitary taxi ride home was better than straining to make basic conversation with strangers or not. Once in the vehicle, she slipped off the mask and conceded to the moist filtered air of the vehicle. Shouting out her home address, she stared at the back of the Robo driver unit. Maybe the unit was recording the ride; she didn't care. The hassle continued in her head. How many times did the doctors kid her in the past, applauding her exercise discipline and positive attitude, "Can't clone that!" Could they manufacture an age busting plasma out of her worthy enzymes?

The cab dropped her off as a heavier downpour took over. She hurried through the pelting rain and kept watch on the debris on the path. Even with her mind swirling in details, once again, she sought to pull something positive from the day. She would read every inch of the new materials. The real news featured pictures of the new greenery and other advanced horticulture experiments in New Florida. If she stayed at the Colony, Riley could disappear off to Denmark. They also prepped her about some recent benefits for being part of a centenarian study if she qualified. Ella paused at the bottom of the elevator and looked up - no lights in Riley's unit. She had time to balance all this out and get her equilibrium back.

CHAPTER 16

A muffled noise greeted Riley as she opened her unit door. It took a few seconds to recognize the sound of Ella thumping something against the laundry/trash shoot - it was a come up ASAP signal. She threw down her bag, and turned right back out to the hallway, went up to the stairs and across the walkway. Almost breathless she fidgeted waiting for Ella to open the door, ready to alert Alvi and get a key. Ella soon appeared her hands up in the air but otherwise looking intact as the door slid open.

"You will not believe. Sorry for the rush."

Out of habit, they went directly to the couch to talk in close proximity. Still, somewhat out of breath, Riley panted, "You gave me a scare. You need to learn to text as you think."

Ella shrugged, "One of these days, I guess. I have so much to tell you." She launched into rehashing her doctor's visit. "The deal is they want me to spend two weeks at the main Institute in Florida. I would finally meet other people in the study. We are supposedly an elite group. They want me to take a train to New Florida and then get on a cruise ship for part of the time. I have to agree to be accompanied the whole time by a staff companion. I met her at my doctor's visit today. Creepy - reminds me of a psych nurse on the mental ward."

Riley's eyes rolled up to the ceiling and down to the floor, "Wait, back it up. Did you say cruise ship? What is the name of the ship? Is it stationed at that Florida port?"

"I didn't ask. They are giving me this information in little nibbles. I didn't know a cruise ship would be part of the deal. I thought I would only be on the main Institute grounds." Ella shifted and glared at Riley, "So much for your plan to take it as it comes."

Riley felt like a child caught doing something wrong and needed to protest her innocence. The barbs of Ella's prickly anger, a rare display from her usually composed friend, threw her off balance. The tension ratcheted back up as Ella continued to look defiant and frightened at the same time. Then Riley decided it was better to let the silence float between them, hoping their raw feelings would settle down. Time to change the subject.

"Well, I have news too. At work, we have been asked to volunteer for short-term assignments at several long-distance sites. I volunteered for the one in New Florida. The timeline is dependent on the weather, maybe two weeks from now. We can be on that same new coast train."

Ella put her arms up in a gesture of victory and took in a quick breath. "At least something is going according to plan." Riley took that as a signal to start barking directions. "You should wrap up all the required paperwork so we can book the same train south."

"But what you saw at the pier, doesn't this add up the wrong way? Now that I have this cruise ship thing being thrown at me, doesn't that change everything?"

Riley paced around the small couch with her hands in her pockets, winding herself tight. She blurted out, "But I will be there with you, we will handle this together even with the cruise ship. Do you trust me? I have survivor skills and contacts in other places."

Ella stayed silent. Riley continued, "I should know more tomorrow at work, they are still sorting out the final roster, but I have a good chance at Denmark as well. Maybe this is the breakthrough we have been waiting for to get beyond our life here and see what is really happening."

"Okay, okay, I get it. Maybe this is exactly what we both been waiting for. Just remember

I will be the one with the lab subject tag in an experiment that I do not know enough about. I may be the one with a price on my head."

Riley took another moment to realize the look on Ella's face had changed again. Her usual trusting smile turned into a firm scowl. She had to offer more reassurance to her doubting friend.

"Well, then we should be prepared to take off before we reach Florida if necessary. Going off the radar may be what is best for both of us."

CHAPTER 17

A week and a half and Alvi had no contact from her parents, no People Time, no texts, and no emails. Her mom had told her in her usual firm but gentle way not to freak out if things went silent.

"This is how it has to be right now; trust me." Alvi moved across the common patio and then started around the building. She checked the power settings, water filtration, and opened the heating and ventilation unit looking for debris. Power storage from the solar collection remained more than adequate despite the gray weather. Solar panels had been fine-tuned to capture any light at any time.

With so many parameters to remember, her mind instead wandered off. Her heart kept sinking farther down into an old well of fear and abandonment. She felt the tightness of her breathing and a quickened heartbeat. A bad taste settled on her tongue. The scared little girl wanted to come out and ruin her day.

It took several minutes to debate her motives and fears and wrestle herself back to a more acceptable level of composure. The possibility of a full-blown panic attack remained an old familiar enemy waiting for its curtain call. The cognitive-behavioral drill ran through her head, what to tell herself, how to force herself to take even measured breaths. In and hold and out. In and hold and out. Best to make an object of herself, study the problem then get to fixing it. It existed as a desperate defense, or maybe a human art form. She was never sure which. Her parents used to refer to the "it will not happen here" game. Combined with the Be Calm and Conquer approach she learned in middle school, she would get through all of this.

The adage repeated in her head: find your quiet space; steady your course and all the other assorted psychobabble messages appropriate from her younger days. She had gone to the school counselor with others for group therapy. Some of them had splintered small bones in their feet from kicking the crap out of inanimate objects. Others had gotten into self-harm to ward off the numbness they felt in a rapidly changing world. Pick another course had been the mantra. Now calm, she wanted to pack a bag and disappear. Duty was duty, but she needed to locate her parents and find out what was happening to her aunt.

With two of her residents going on trips that would last at least two weeks, she could notify Harold's CCR and ask for a backup for him. Everyone equated traveling with potential danger from weather and non-colonized parts of the country. Maybe she could text that guy from her last class who went south regularly and ask a few questions. People made up urban legends of marauding bands of misfits attacking anything that came through their territory. It was her prerogative to call in a caretaker sub for a few days, a kind of emergency family travel leave as long as the remaining residents had someone to reach. Completing that next level of thought soothed her down another notch. So what if it broke her perfect record. Better to make it through the next few days and try to reach her sister Maya again.

Maya had extensive travel privileges as a journalist and seemed to know where the trouble spots were. She told Alvi tales of different renegade groups of people who traveled in old solar hybrid buses and took over abandoned malls or any weather worthy structures as they headed to the western states. Some wanted to bond together over their beliefs about the end of the world, and others only wanted to spend their forever-imminent final days in peace. Others of a more violent nature armed themselves against becoming part of the new normal. Each group believed their calling above the law, and declared putting all this order in disorder a farce. That made them justify taking what was not theirs. The Real News broadcasted their known locations, mapping them as sinkholes labeled Live Free and Die.

Part of the west coast had turned into pockets of discontent each with its agenda. Maybe a trip down the carved out eastern seaboard was not as dangerous. Her parents would not risk this trip unless her aunt was dying. She put out a special message through the Next of Kin channel. Maya would not be able to ignore her any longer.

CHAPTER 18

Harold inched his way along the wall with one hand, gripping his cane in the other until he met the back of his chair. Getting around to the front of it would require more time and caution if he was to stay on his feet. Finally, he let himself sink slowly into the waiting arms of the overstuffed divan. The trembling had stopped. He waited as his heart rate shifted back to semi-normal. The grim reality of what just happened washed over him.

Crossing the room a few moments ago to look down at the courtyard, he felt lightheaded and did not possess his legs. They were underneath him but useless. Blood pressure must be off, that could be it. His pressure cuff was right there on the side table, but he did not want to know. He was able to get to the sturdiness of the furniture before the hardness of the floor. This was a save for now. He fingered his mobile alert response system in his pocket but didn't summon help. A few months ago, he tried that and had to go through days of scrutiny. He never mentioned it to Colin, though they probably sent him a notice.

All the commotion years ago about holistic living never suited him. He had lived his life his way for all his 93 years. His last wife died over 20 years ago, so he had no one in his everyday life to nag him about the new rules of living longer than you wanted to. He turned off his music and brooded over his options. Doors were not opening. They were closing; it was as simple as that. Maybe it was time to look into an old offer if he could find that web page again. He had memorized a nickname for the website, the silver slide. It was a society, an organization, but he could not place the formal title. The promo started with a deep, reassuring voice, "How do you want to spend your last days when that time comes for you..." The Society used technology and medical science to predict your oncoming death within weeks and days. "So choose where you want to spend your final time. It can be somewhere you have never been or your favorite place in the world. We will assure that you are comfortable and not alone. Your privacy is utmost for us." Harold understood the promise; death will not sneak up on you like a clumsy burglar. You do not want to be found days, weeks after your remains contaminate the floor.

The prospect of Colin and his family moving farther away would mean a deeper level of scrutiny from the Colony caretaker and other authorities. How could he guilt his grandnephew for making a major move? Colin had done more for him then perhaps a son or grandson. There was still money to pass on, and the beneficiaries were laid out in his will. Even this moderate sum would make a difference to Colin in protecting his young family, a little extra padding in this hard knock life. He was calm now; he reconnected his headphones and sailed into the middle of one of his favorite choral pieces. The beauty of the voices always enveloped him in the comfort of his pampered past.

Yes, it was all a matter of symmetry; you have to write the ending well. Maybe a few last experiences while he waited for final arrangements would be a good idea. He was way past anything dramatic like hang gliding even if they had that anymore. The old archives had visual treats of unspoiled wonders of the world. What he wanted was a time capsule to go back, be in the middle of his life before the world fell apart and possess the wisdom he had found in maturity of his ending days. He would have treated people better, made some of his students value their worth more than how high they could sing in an octave.

At least he could ask young Alvi about those concert tickets again. He would visit the nice younger older woman on the next floor down. In his few encounters with his neighbors, she was always a friendly face. Time to breathe some different air, just huddling like a bear hibernating in his cave seemed the wrong thing to do. At some point, you knew what you have left and how you want to spend it. He switched to the classic hard rock part of his playlist and swayed a little as the guitar riff infused new energy at least in his mind. With a much shorter future ahead of him, he would only ask one more thing of life. Tomorrow he would plan his path.

The next morning he woke up with a sense of purpose. Harold leaned forward on his cane and peered in the dimness of his closet. Somewhere in the back, he had stored his old environ suit. He felt stronger when he woke up. Maybe this was a day to go somewhere, do something. Getting it out of the closet, and even the idea of how to get into it quickly became too much of a struggle. The weather app showed partly stormy weather followed by moderate winds. All he had to do was go out to the corridor and down the elevator and over to Ella's unit. He whined to himself, how can you be spontaneous and visit a neighbor when you need preparations befitting a mountain expedition?

He shuffled back over to the desk. A visual tour of the canals in Venice with a coordinated concert of Handel's Water Music would be soothing right now. He closed his eyes and sat back to absorb the familiar tones. A flash of memory sped by him. His gaze drifted up to the bookcase wall. Holding his cane by the end, he reached across with the curved handle and brushed along the spines of the books. He hooked a likely candidate, pulling it out and down. The volume tumbled down and landed in the middle of the desk. He thumbed through the cover jacket and the pages. No dice. Up again he tried for another, then down. By the third attempt, the room was starting to dance around him. The frustration pushed him on.

Well, old man, you think you are so smart, why didn't I copy it down? Which book did you pick to keep it so safe from prying eyes? He cursed at himself. Silver bookmark for the silver slide...or was it a silver scoop. No way could he search in his email stream from two years back. The day he let the representative into his unit, the man had handed him an old-style paper bookmark as a business card. They were talking about fate, being passive, or deciding your finale. The rep told about Clotho, one of the three fates in Greek Mythology.

Yes! He poked out with his cane again and connected with the maroon leather volume from the bottom shelf. It landed with the spine up on the side of the desk. He took a moment to steady himself, and then opened it with a slight theatrical flair. He cleared his throat, "We have a winner," he shouted out. He saw a flash of the ornate metallic paper nestled in the crease of the pages among the richly engraved illustrations of the ancient gods and goddesses. He took a moment to admire the beauty of the old embossed print on paper then placed the bookmark just above his keyboard. The words Klotho Society floated up, reassuring him that yes, he had found the beginning of the right path.

He swiveled in the chair to look at the rest of the room. It was a genuinely odd sort of excitement, a glint of his own vanity. It has always been a matter of pride, making the right decisions at the right time, about his career, his marriages, and divorces. He recognized all the physical signs, no need for another visit to his doctor to tell him what he already knew. Being out of breath, sleeping longer, that is what most of his days were now. Losing his memory and not being in charge of what life he had left had always been his worst fear. Now an internal countdown, some innate part stalked him, the messages clear in its urgency.

The strength in his mind wrapped tightly around the weakness in his body as his breathing steadied. He would set up a call on the encrypted channel as he did before. The Society already had a copy of his will, but they would want to know his bank account balance. He glanced again around the unit and took a mental inventory of the few material pieces of his long-ordered life. In the morning, he should start to pack for the trip, but enough for now. He was in charge again; in charge of what time he had left. Dying should not be just a passive afterthought. Why wait for the fates to decide when and where the thread of your life should break?

PART TWO

NEW FLORIDA
BOUND

CHAPTER 19

Ella welcomed the motion of the train as somehow both familiar and strange. The soothing rhythm of rocking sideways while moving forward reassured her. This train had much more to offer than being anchored to the earth and safe from violent weather. It presented a window to miles of the deadened landscape interrupted by brilliant outbursts of human activity. A lot of that was blue tarps and old trailers, but it spoke of a constant band of reconstruction. Living along the train lines had become a new lifeline for many. New age climate housing modules sprouted like so many do-it-yourself projects. There were groups of people raising small houses gathered under the protection of massive reinforced run off roofs. This is what she wanted to see — proof of other people's courage to make a new start.

The heavy rains acted differently at this speed, rivets of water cascaded backward as if you could actually outrun the weather and leave it behind. The broad doublewide train was roomier but quieter than her commuting days. The gentler sound resembled a giant battery-run toy with a low soft pitch. When the shrill signal blew, Ella longed for an old-style whistle to trail behind puffing out a muffled wail. This hydrogen battery version emitted an odd signal announcing the stops and starts of the journey. The sound resonated like a giant fire truck with a get out of the way warning. The travel log stated it would take over fifty hours to arrive in the middle of what remained above the sea rise line in the rehabbed state of Florida. Driving there remained a possibility for those who could afford constant protection along the way. On her map, the Institute for Longevity sat on the grounds of a former childhood entertainment complex.

There would be interesting stops along the way. Riley had managed to book this same train for a work trip. She had marked where she wanted to meet to compare notes. Riley approached this trip as if the enemy tracked them both, again not clear who that might be. Ella was beginning to realize that her friend missed her earlier days of underground activism. There always had to be a plan to move your cause forward, Riley could never let herself believe that progress was happening without cost.

She glanced to her left. Mattie, her health/ med companion from the study group, was implanted beside her. Since leaving several hours ago, Ella actively resisted the creeping sense of being an escorted prisoner. The woman knew how to be acceptable company, but she cringed at the amount of her own personal medical detail this health wellness expert tossed about so freely. Is this what it was like to have an enthusiastic but somehow deranged fan club? She gushed about how Ella's health parameters were so superior for someone her age.

"It is so rare to see someone improve their bone density! I had five people recheck your T scores to prove it." Mattie tilted sideways in her seat and clapped her hands together lightly. Ella forced a smile and tried to ignore the performance beside her.

"Well, my Osteo doc told me years ago to follow the Japanese method of standing on one leg at a time to build up my hip bone density." Ella half expected her to pull out a notebook but realized that somehow she was recording their every interaction. Mattie's wristband device was oversized for her small wrist.

"And keeping such a consistent diet all these years, even before offending foods disappeared, you are a marvel."

Mattie prattled on with a whole litany of the simple wellness practices Ella held over the years as if she knew every shred of her daily routine, and every illness. She wondered if Mattie knew why she was infertile forty years ago. She had understood that filling out all those surveys over the years for the Longevity Study made her an open book and perhaps a genuine public spectacle all along. Right now, the full realization of what she had already given away sunk in hard.

Ella tried to put on a smile, and asked, "What about your own health routines, tell me what you think is important." She would at least attempt to change the focus back to Mattie. For a few minutes, Mattie slipped from a hyperactive focus on her charge and talked about her inverted yoga routine. Ella swallowed a laugh and hid a sneer at the same time. All that blood running to your head. Then Mattie resumed her role as keeper of the order and brought the conversation back to Ella and her base conditioning. "Your lab tests mirror someone almost twenty years younger." Ella consoled herself with the fact that she was neither an egotist nor a narcissist. She joined the study to contribute to medical knowledge and simply because a friend asked her. Whatever else she accomplished to keep her ahead of the aging curve just through exercise, discipline, or a genetic component, she owned only as a happy mystery.

Weary of this, Ella positioned her head to look like she was listening. Filtering through the bits of information that Mattie batted out, she only wanted to hear a more specific reason as to why the study had singled her out for this trip besides the fact she had met some elite standards for staying younger. Was she finally going to meet other advanced study members like herself? Was there to be a pageant complete with cash prizes? She would ask, but Mattie had the hard veneer of don't ask me, I won't tell you.

Her thoughts sneaked off to double task on other things. Before they left, Ella had confirmed that there would be others on the train in her age group. She needed to find time to seek them out and loosen herself from Mattie's web. The only other passengers she had seen in the last few hours were mostly couples who couldn't seem to keep their hands off each other. "Mattie, is this a lover's lane, why so many young couples?"

"New Florida is a journey people make for a wide range of reasons, kind of a cradle to the grave option." Ella blinked and turned away. Then Mattie muttered something about meeting up with others like her down the line. Ella wanted to know if they were wrestling with her dilemma. Only a select few of the Institute's subjects were being spoon-fed additional untested ingredients for longer life. Again, she felt guilt and greed. Why was she so fortunate to be aging so well? What would happen to her if she abruptly stopped all of this? What if in the end, she did not meet the Institute's expectations.

All this isolated special treatment made her feel less like a preferred customer who won a free holiday and more like a specimen facing an expiration date. She was not going to find it sitting here next to this walking talking health database.

That morning, as she got into the jitney to the local to the central train station, Ella looked back at her colony building, her home for over a decade. Her neighbor had agreed to check on the watering system for her plants. She packed only the allowed 30-pounds of baggage. It was a series of tough decisions. What could she leave behind if she was never to come back? What if she and Riley headed off for parts unknown? She hoped that at no point would security open her bag in front of her official companion. It would be awkward to explain some of her oldest keepsakes she brought for what is supposed to be only a fourteen-day round trip. Her sister's music box would seem a bit out of place. The day before leaving, she and Riley congratulated themselves on managing to get booked on the same train leaving on the same day to go most of the way to their separate destinations in New Florida. A patch of decent weather naturally synchronized their trips. You go when you can go.

Early this morning she had met Riley briefly downstairs to lay out a plan to try to contact each other on the train without drawing attention. They both gave Alvi plausible reasons they would be away from their units and their expected return dates. They were not obliged to say where they were going, just a period for their units to power down and save energy. Being away too long without explanation, they could risk forfeiting their units, as there were long waiting lists for such protected housing. Riley mentioned that Alvi did not seem to give her long absence a second thought.

"Our usually vigilant caretaker seemed very distracted. I am surprised she did not ask any real questions. I could be away at least a month, and she did not react at all."

"I sent a simple email explaining about the study through the longevity panel, and that was it. I didn't even get a response besides that fact she received it." With a somber tone of regret in her voice, Ella added, "If leaving to travel was this easy, maybe we should have made some shorter trips before this."

"You forget, I travel all the time," Riley shot back.

"Yes, but only in state... this is equivalent of crossing a country's border. I am surprised we did not need passports."

They compared notes on the logistics of the trip and where, when, and how they could communicate on the train. What used to be a 22-hour overnight trip straight down the eastern seaboard to Miami, now drew a zigzag course farther inland and with more stops for more extended periods. The train path paralleled the contours of the new coastline with promises about being able to explore some of the rebuilt cities like New Charlestown and New Savannah. They advertised beautiful attractions, no danger, no harm. Final stop, Lakeland, nestled safely in the center of Florida and from there they both had other connections, but they would be within blocks of each other.

"I am special. I have a sleeping berth," teased Ella. Riley deadpanned her answer as if made no difference. "I will sit in the lounge section as much as I can. As long as I can walk up and down the aisles, I will be ok. I have some coding prep to do with Lindy."

"I will be careful not to say anything around your coworker if we do meet up in the aisles," promised Ella. Then she pushed back further against Riley's wall of paranoia. "Really who cares, we are neighbors that happen to be going the same way, at the same time. Everything does not have a sinister meaning."

"Yes, but if you have to break away from your keeper, we do not want her to associate me with you. I do not want my employer knowing I may want to stay in Europe if I get there. They have lost a few workers over the years to the better conditions there. We could even end up in Denmark and start a whole new life." Ella chose not to go further with that thought.

"Once we are in Lakeland, Lindy and I have a shuttle to Tampa to a conference center. By then, I will know more about whether I go on to the Denmark assignment. The weather window does not have anything dramatic in it so far. They built this new train system well. The doublewide cars can withstand storms, so everything should be relatively on schedule. Cell communication will be crappy as usual." They made tentative plans to be in the dining car at the same time, but Ella warned it would be difficult to separate from her health advisor. "She is even going to watch my diet."

CHAPTER 20

Riley leaned over and rested her head against the train window. The vibrations pulsed in her ear. Lindy had managed to book upper-level seats in the wide window car. She felt less claustrophobic sitting here at the top of the train. The full see-through floor to ceiling Plexiglas window was scratched and dull, but it opened up to a sky morphing from blues to grays to full clouds. On the ground, there were changes out there to see if you cared to pay attention. Riley thought of it as confirmation of what she had seen in the media. With the climate migration from coastal cities and swept away flatlands, old rural communities kept turning into bustling towns. Building, rehabbing, and growth were happening everywhere.

The coding work could only keep her in her seat so long. The changing terrain matched up with her restless mood as she stared out the window. The reality of having to sit for long hours was her foe. Her legs should be pumping as best they can on a bike pointed where she wanted to go. If she didn't stretch, her joint pain would be unbearable when she got up. Riley checked her bag again. She brought along a decent batch of anti-flam pills. She tapped her foot against the bottom of the seat in front of her. Lindy had been gone for over half an hour. They still had more coding assignments to do before the cyber conference. Prep was important when you were vying to outperform other teams for a few of the more exciting travel slots. Riley tabbed through some of the complex protocols on her tablet. Even without a full IT degree, Riley held her own in these programming skirmishes. Her company recognized her Gordian knot level of patience in solving impasses.

Lindy had brimmed with excitement as they left but was spending a lot her time on her cell while still in range. Just as she tilted out into the aisle, she could see Lindy swaying towards her. She landed firmly in the seat and let out a long slow sigh of relief. "That was ridiculous; just getting to the toilet is a three-car expedition. The cell coverage is still crappy, but at least they have a map showing better spots along the route."

Riley did not bother to acknowledge her complaint at first. The less she talked the less chance she would start up about her sinister plot thoughts as Ella called them. Riley had finally learned not to wear her politics on her sleeve that covered her fading anti-fa tattoos. Ella knew not to use the expression 'conspiracy theories' around her unless she wanted to be dragged back twenty-plus years when they were all over the media. Riley thought twice about it and managed to think herself into a smile and a passable comment.

"I am sure as we get closer to the new city stops and Florida and you will have a better connection."

Riley had already accepted that this was going to be a whole lot of closeness with someone only marginally agreeable, but that was how Riley classified most people. To her surprise, Lindy leaned over and spoke in a whisper, "Someone is selling mood pills in the car just past the dining one." Riley whipped off her headphones, stared at Lindy, and found herself almost shouting. "How do you know they are what they are advertising?"

"I just saw a transaction and asked. They are happy face buttons, endorphin pills."

"And you bought some?" Lindy returned a why not gesture. Riley considered being the wiser older adult to push back against Lindy's impulse buy. "They are the ones good for a quick pick me up...they aren't addictive, and this is the closest thing I get to a vacation mode, don't lecture me."

Riley went back to her usual cone of silence. Ok then, fine with her, she didn't want it to lead to a conversation about her use in her twenties of more potent substances. She tried to sound casual. "You do what you want to do, as long as you can code when we get to Florida."

The sticky labyrinth of her past life made Riley assume that things could turn to crap with even the simplest of decisions. She acknowledged that rule probably applied to her life more than others did. All the twists and turns in her life came from bad luck and bad timing, along with limited choices. Riley envied the simplicity of her coworker's path through the jungle of the last twenty years; she could fall into a sewer and come out with presentation roses. In her early forties now, Lindy already had a degree before all the changes, and then somehow stepped into a stable corporate job. Lindy never had to move from her original home area because of a monstrous climate event. She was also young enough to have support medically and financially in her decision to become a single mom a dozen years ago. While others stumbled and fell into pits of doubt and self-destruction, Lindy never lost a step in her personal and work ambitions.

To Lindy's credit, Riley had never seen her treat good fortune with an air of complacency. As Riley glanced over, Lindy was smiling to herself. She had to admit it was worthwhile to know someone at work as positive as Lindy. No one could say she chose to have children just for the support and privileges it afforded her. Lindy believed in the future. Riley was still working on the future part.

As she watched, Lindy leaned back even further in her seat and floated off on the chemical cloud passing through her system. Unable to cross her long legs, Riley just bounced her knees together, then side to side. Again, she checked the time, too early to go to the dining car. Around noon, she would try for a casual encounter with Ella after cautioning Ella not to text her. She wanted to operate this trip like a logical piece of code. First A and then B and if not C, then on to D.

Ella's idea was to find other people to acknowledge that their fears had a concrete basis and then work together to find a solution or an escape. She reasoned that if there was some kind of subversive plot removing older citizens, being very paranoid and isolating yourself was not going to help. If it was real, someone had to expose it. Ella was no longer saying it's all in your head, not after the scene at the dock.

She wanted – needed to protect Ella, the woman who took her from temp status at their old company into something resembling a real job. Ella helped her get into the colony housing. After coming to the company on a part-time basis, Ella was the one who paid enough attention to the new recruit on her project to know something was wrong. Others ignored her or passed her off as quirky at best, morose at worse. She was more publicly outspoken then, and her break room rants were forceful about how things had to change faster. She had gone beyond the status of weekend protest warrior that others indulged in. All the fight she had when she was younger was now energy escaping in fighting her physical pain. Doctors had not been able to explain why she was losing steam. She felt lost without the power to move forward. That day she had felt somehow just suspended in midair just waiting for something to push her one way or the other. Ella read her like a book and made a direct invite to come home with her for dinner after work. Riley remembered making eye contact and knowing her temp boss would not take no for an answer.

It had been the start of a strange but sincere friendship. Even in Ella's small unit in this weird building, Riley saw someone who believed things would get better. This crazy woman thought she could still grow plants. She had shown Riley the tiniest of seeds in the palm of her hand. They were smaller than a grain of salt that would grow into a tall shaggy Indian Peace Pipe flower. They failed as the perennials they were supposed to be, but Ella restarted the plants every year telling Riley that she was someone who believed in beating the odds. Despite the hard-concrete exterior of her bunker as Riley called it, she found someone who listened to her and shared her separate losses. Riley gained from Ella that you can lose much and still be bold and want more out of life. Ella listened to her rants about how much the world still needed to change even as things were starting to transform at light speed. That night when she sat across from Ella at the table set with real china and actual fresh greens to augment their rations, something pushed a measure of her despair back into a quiet corner. She sat facing someone who had her own sad story to tell but who believed all the changes would amount to something. Ella admitted that when it came to the political stuff, she had not risked much. She had gone to the dollar store and bought poster boards to make other people signs, then hid them from her husband.

She had been a spectator and a silent cheerleader at first.

Riley shared tales of some of her more violent encounters and explained some of her line tattoos. While Ella put markers to poster board, Riley had her beliefs needled into her skin. Their connection grew simply by both of them accepting and endorsing the actions of the other. Riley felt less like she lived on her own remote part of the planet. Back then, she needed to find more reasons for living and fewer excuses for taking the easy way out of a hard life. She did not know why, but at the end of that first dinner, she had gone home and thrown away the sleeping pills she had stored in an old backpack.

Ella infused her view that the more time you have, the more time you can hope for change. That was over a decade ago, and change had come for Riley in a steadier job, and a housing unit that would not disappear on her. Ella had helped her with all of it. For the first time since being a young adult, she had a stable place to live. This newer improved version of her life did not require as much energy. Ella pointed her to some pain amelioration clinics and wellness techniques that helped her aching body. Now she was the one trying to guide Ella's fate.

She talked Ella into saying yes to this trip for the Institute, knowing they could travel together. If things went sour, she still had some tenuous connections to the old underground activist network. Ella had accepted her untested promise, stick with me, and it will be all right. What if she messed up big time and Ella ended up turning into a set of test tubes for the Institute?

CHAPTER 21

Riley fidgeted in her seat and rechecked the time, 12:05. The dining car would be crowded. She stepped over Lindy and headed towards the stairwell down to the main cars. As she reached the third car back and stood in the connecting corridor, she allowed several people to pass. She spotted Ella with a bouncy little woman glued to her side coming from the other direction. Riley moved slowly towards them, so she could stand close to Ella as others in the line took turns going into the dining car. She had a small folded note in her hand and managed an almost flawless one-handed pass. Ella smirked as she felt something in her pocket. In response, Ella gave a simple hand signal to show nothing new so far from her travel companion. When Mattie turned, Riley watched as Ella rolled her eyes and silently mouthed the words, "You have been watching too many old spy dramas."

As they finally entered the dining car, a happy buzz of voices came from the front of the line. "They have lemons...and chocolate!" The menu for the mid-day meal hung high on the wall, written in chalk on an old-style black-board. Even with one 'choice' being provided as part of their fare, this seemed less like being in a soup kitchen. On the top of the board, today's offering - The Best Vegetarian Chili in the World. A pleasant smell wafted forward from behind the counter. Riley sat close by and watched Ella's face, full of excitement as she peered down into her bowl. Her friend ladled out three different types of beans, small corn-cobs, and red and yellow peppers. She examined them like a botanist in a lab...fresh then frozen, amazing. Also beside everyone's bowl was an ice-cube size portion of cornbread. Ella rolled her eyes again in Riley's direction this time as if to say, you will not believe how good this is. Everyone seemed to be in awe of this tasty combination, and ate with slow reverence, relishing the variety of tastes. The iced tea came with a wedge of lemon on the edge of the cup. People were sniffing it and rubbing it on their tongues.

Mattie started up with a grievance: "They really should list if this is gluten-free." Ella did not even pretend she was listening. How could you argue about such a bona fide feast? In another minute, even Mattie stopped talking and consumed the meal. She heard Mattie comment about how they must be growing the lemons somewhere outside again. The chocolate promised on the menu turned out to be a small wrapped portion of the 70% dark cocoa bar. "Not to everyone's taste – more bitter than sweet," Mattie complained. Ella put some little extra bars in her pocket when Mattie looked the other way. Who needed a food critic when real food sat in front of you? This was a small food revolution. Someone was growing not synthesized peppers and real beans. She took each piece of the cooked peppers and savored it individually on her tongue. Someone had accomplished a yield far higher than her pampered patio garden. Plant life was budding somewhere.

CHAPTER 22

After Ella and Mattie filed back to their seats, Riley remained in the dining car. She finished everything on her tray and then started back the opposite way. The travel app that came with her ticket promised all sorts of activities in the non-passenger sections of the train. In the next car, people were jammed together on the open bench seats watching a live performance. The show consisted of a talented guitarist and a vocalist at the front of the car taking requests. From the vibe in the crowd, she guessed they were making a decent job of it. Hearing someone sing Elton John's "Goodbye Yellow Brick Road" seemed to mesmerize the audience.

The motion of the train, along with the rhythm of the instruments, made Riley want to linger. The applause broke out behind her as she continued through to the passageway. Somehow, it was a startling sound to hear, so human and spontaneous. At the start of the next car, a whiteboard announced an open comedy mic within the next hour. She found herself looking out at the vistas passing by. The pallor of the morning was gone, the sky was almost clear but still streaked with clouds, and the mountains were visible at a distance. Above one mountain, she saw the combination of a small batch of blue peeking out as a crystal blue iris nestled in a patch of white staring at her. At home, this would have seemed ominous; here, it somehow fit with the landscape that was ushering them along. A speaker by her head coughed out a broken up message. They would soon be going over a bridge. Riley remained longer at the window as a lake with tiny islands came into view. She guessed that twenty years ago, this was a cozy little town in a valley. Maybe someday she would see things in reference to the future, not the past.

Riley climbed the second set of stairs to a separate upper viewing car and was surprised to see just more travelers, no real first-class partitions. The extra money for the upper seating must be for the view. If there was a VIP section on this train, it had to be located somewhere else. Having walked the length of that car, she turned back and descended the same staircase. She was like a bird foraging for crumbs. The good mood of the well-fed and entertained passengers kept chipping away at her perennial lousy mood. She had seen strangers relaxed together in the safe confines of this traveling roadshow. No wonder people saved up to take this trip as often as they could. She pressed on through the wellness cars with no seating except for two curtained off medical areas. The next car featured treadmills and recumbent bikes. People were taking numbers, waiting patiently, and talking. With all this jabbering, her self-styled isolation weighed her down like a medieval suit of armor. The next car stood almost empty with no immediate purpose, and then another dining car just past it.

A momentary weakness in her knees pressed her towards an empty row of seats. She could lay down for a short while and take the chance the occupants would not return. She stretched out and rested her head, looking out the window. As she pulled back, she caught her reflection. Her purple hair and the trailing ends of her neck tattoo stood out but only for a moment. The puffy bags hung under her eyes, and worry lines wrote volumes across her forehead. Ella told her years ago that her mouth was stuck in a permanent pout. She fought the urge to make sour faces at herself. Instead, she studied the train map. There were ten more cars to search for what she wasn't sure, and then she should go back to her seat. Her bloodhound instincts were looking for trouble or evidence of someone being oppressed right now, and she was growing weary.

As people started returning from the forward dining car, Riley pulled herself up, winced as the persistent pain in her hips tried to pull her back down. She realized the folly of hoping to overhear some useful conversations. This was a party train, not a death train. Life did not seem threatened here. Maybe she was overwrought after all. Riley let it sink in. All her talk and warnings had unsettled her very well settled friend. All she could confirm at this point was that many people just took this train trip south for the respite it gave from being encased in their climate colonies with nothing but work and home. The laughter and the conversations of the other passengers jeered at her to enjoy the ride. She had heard more hopeful things than not. People were making plans about schooling, about bringing family members back together.

Maybe just being out of their home colonies and feeling secure on this fortified train endorsed a sense of adventure and discovery lacking in everyday life. When you spent most of the time inside dodging storms, having plans canceled, the train ride was a simple, reliable schedule with time to relate to others, to hear what was happening somewhere besides your little corner of the world. Riley knew she fought optimism as if it was a wet blanket, ready to smother her reason and resolve. Now upbeat thoughts were starting to peek out from under her safety net of precautions. She was losing her internal debate to keep her negative radar up and running. Maybe Ella could simply follow through with whatever exams the Longevity Institute had in store for her and go back to the colony, no harm done. She passed a group of teenagers in the next two cars heading back to the entertainment cars.

"Hey, look, a real farm." Riley turned and saw a series of sheltered farming growhouses. Massive machines were spring seeding the newly turned earth inside the structures. Everyone in the car followed the farming activity as the train passed miles of fields. Passengers were pressing to one side of the car. Riley listened to their revelry about reinvented farming.

"Did you see that silo and the huge barns?" There even was a momentary nodding of heads and small cheers.

"Maybe this is where part of our lunch came from," someone called out beside her. Riley sneered in their direction; this younger set was easily impressed. She was not about to applaud the reinvention of something that never should have disappeared in the first place.

As the two-parent types took their seats, Riley moved in a little closer "Yeah, I can barely remember, but my grandpa had a farm before the drought, and the tornadoes made it a dust bowl. When I was little, he put some dark rich earth in my hand and said that there is one thing you never make more of - land."

"Where did he end up after all that?

"Well he went to live with my aunt, but about two years ago he just packed a bag and left without a trace."

Riley stopped for a moment. It was not unlike other stories she had heard. She could file this under ... and then? She did not let it nag at her right now. As others returned to their seats, Riley pushed on through the last few cars until she came to a Do Not Enter / Authorized Personnel Only sign. Something about a sign like this always engaged her spirit. Right now she needed to go back and make sure Lindy had not drifted too far off planet earth. She turned and passed back through several cars. As she entered the next connecting platform, someone stood to the side of the area. Instead of moving on, she stopped and faced the back of the figure. He remained motionless with his legs planted firmly between the steel panels where the steps would go down. Something made her wait there and watch the stillness of his body. His bowed head rose slowly above his shoulders as he sensed she was not moving.

As he turned around to face her, Riley sucked in a short breath. It was like looking in a mirror, a reflection of herself in a male body, maybe in his early fifties but weary-looking. His shoulders were hunched over and his hair and beard brown but in a transition stage of motley gray. His hands stuck tightly in his pockets as he used his feet for balance. On his bare forearm, she recognized a familiar but faded line tattoo proclaiming owning the future. The look on his face broadcast clearly, she was not welcome. He attempted to dislodge her scrutiny of him with the glare of someone who would not take no for an answer and wanted the unwelcome intruder to move on. She matched his glare with her own; I am not going anywhere stance. His surface anger melted into a weary concentration. Now she stared back into the pooled sadness of his brown eyes. Those eyes suggested a different truth to her; he was positioning himself to throw himself under the train. The conductors did not always secure the steps guards. It would take some effort, but if determined, you could grab the railing that

helped passengers disembark and swing yourself down to a swift death under the grinding
wheels as they came into a station. Riley edged
back as far as she could in her side of the small
space. He took a single step towards her and
stood directly under the dim light in the roof
of the passageway. She sensed he was measur-
ing his words and braced herself for a string
of profanity. Instead, the silence stretched out
longer. Riley realized he was checking her out
physically in a way that had not occurred in at
least a decade or two. Thrown off guard, she
lashed out by being the first to speak.

"You really could botch it up you know and
end up a double amputee."

The force of her delivery and its clear message, made him step back. She assumed he was
struggling with the right comeback, not too
flippant, angry, or dismissive. Her intrusion
had brought him back from somewhere very
dark.

"Do you always go around trying to read
people's minds?" he spat out.

Finally, she thought, we are getting somewhere.

"Well, I just do not want to see you disap-
pointed."

Her snapback felt right, somewhere between aloof and callous. Her eyes met his again

and gave away her concern. He took another step back but still faced her. He knew now she was not going away.

"You can go now. I won't do anything rash. I want to see New Charleston first."

Riley stood firm. She wanted more time with this bookend from the past. She decided to call his bluff, "Ok, so what is so great about New Charleston?"

He shot her another dubious look, as to say why you are bothering me, why should I bother with you. He started to stand a little straighter and pushed his shoulders back, maybe an attempt to look more together or taller, she couldn't tell.

This time, he tried a more casual tone. "They planned ahead and moved a lot of the city's legacy stuff inland and recreated the second city before the flooding." He started to sound like a seasoned tour guide and prattled on about moving giant porch swings and forts and other historical spots. Riley felt an inner flush of confusion. She had been wrong in throwing suicidal intent at him. Now he was throwing a completely different ball in her court.

Then as if they had met on an online dating site, he asked, "Do you want to walk the city with me? They give us a 50-minute layover. There is plenty of security there."

A faint shy smile spread ever so slowly across his face that washed out Riley's fear that he had a screw loose. She answered, almost stuttering. "Ok sounds... good."

He opened the door to the next compartment either to be old-style mannerly or to follow her in the same direction. She looked over her shoulder, and he was right there. Unclear as to what to do next, she felt light-headed. Was he bluffing? After giving her quick directions on where to meet when the train pulled in, he veered in the opposite direction back through the cars.

She stood there for a moment, reoriented herself and continued back to make her way down through the cars. The entertainment cars were full of laughter and applause, and her mood buoyed along the surface. She found Lindy staring out the window, bored, with her work tablet in her lap. Riley thought about sharing about her confrontation with the stranger but held it close. Somehow, what just happened felt very private, very personal? It was a strange sensation as if someone had ripped off her emotional armor then handed her a warm puppy.

She climbed awkwardly over Lindy to her window seat. It didn't matter. They already had separate plans for each train layover so they could spend time apart. Riley pulled out the small cloth pillow that was wedged in the pocket of the seat in front of her. She flipped the tab to inflate it and pushed it into the crack between her seat back and the window. She tried to ignore the vinyl smell. Sunshine was finding its way in through the stormproof glass, no UV rays but real on your face warmth. Her head oriented towards it like a solar panel seeking the sun. Two more hours until the train pulled in, time for a long nap.

She had encountered a puzzle in this person. She knew she was not always good at reading people, but she knew somehow that this guy had more of a story to tell. Besides this nameless creature reminded her of earlier times, it was worth to risk to seek out someone who might understand her for who she was.

CHAPTER 23

Ella opened her eyes just enough to confirm Mattie was not next to her. Maybe her pretend nap was working again and she had some options to explore the train. Uncurling her body and stretching her legs across the other seat, she took in a long breath and let it out slowly. Trying to hide her level of annoyance all this time, took a toll. Her head and heart were in protective mode even with the woman out of her sight. This level of scrutiny was suffocating. She felt justified in what she was about to do. It is my life; my decision and she will not hijack my freedom. Ella pulled her light jacket out of the carry-on bag, slipped it on, and put the hood up. She was reasonably sure Mattie had gone to the rear restroom. As she started to stand, to head in the opposite direction, she grabbed the mini plastic map at the last moment from her front seat pocket. She had seen Mattie slip her tablet deep in the adjoining pocket. Maybe this was her chance to find her file on the company device. Ella felt exhilarated and motivated all at the same time. Mattie had quietly imputed information as they traveled these last hours. Ella sat sideways towards the window and hunched over the device. Fortunately, the Institute had not sprung for the more expensive AI tech protections.

Riley's paranoia was in her head as she joked to herself, I should be wearing gloves, or they will find my biometrics on the keys. She swiped, and the password access box appeared. She quickly keyed in several combinations. Over these last few hours each time she saw Mattie log in, she tried to catch the first and last entries. She hoped to get creative and fill in the middle...kind of like that old game show. At least she could duplicate what she had seen Mattie do. No luck. She sighed and placed it back exactly as she found it and tumbled out in the aisle to make her temporary escape.

Her heartbeat slowed by the time she passed forward into the third car, and she had not run back into Mattie. She straightened her shoulders and pushed the hood back. She felt like a rabbit running from a fox. She was not sure where Riley was sitting; her covert note had not bothered to give her that necessary information. As she entered the next car, she scanned the back of the heads of the passengers, hoping to spot Riley's short cut and purple tint.

No gray heads, again there were mostly young couples. On to the next car, she stopped short when she saw two figures hunched over a tablet. One was an older head, complete with silver mane; she passed them and turned slightly.

Ella froze and took in a short breath. "Tess?"

The two figures looked up and over at her standing in the aisle. The younger woman did not scowl but was not happy with the intrusion. The older woman stared at her through a thin fog of momentary confusion. Ella beamed, waiting for a response. Finally, the seated woman burst out, "My Ella!" The woman rose to her feet with some difficulty, and reached out and grabbed Ella like a life preserver. They stood there together, just grinning and confirming their good fortune to be in the same place at the same time. Ella filled the next few minutes with dates, names, and locations explaining to the younger woman their long history. They had gone to school together and found each other years later and been neighbors. After the death of Tess's husband, both of them had moved away.

"...And she was the one who talked me into signing up for this study.... We lost track of each other ...this is such a thrill." By this time, Ella was so animated that the young woman, obviously a Mattie clone from the same Institute,

gave up trying to guide the conversation. Determined to release her old friend for some private time, Ella thought of an excuse.

"I was just going for some time in the gym
car, can she join me?"

"You keep saying I need to do more," Tess
prodded her companion. "I promise to be back
shortly."

The woman crossed her arms but was de-
feated by the power of the dual force in front
of her. Reluctantly she just nodded, and they
moved to the next car before speaking in the
passageway, "It is too noisy in here. Let's go
up to the other level." Tess agreed, but Ella
realized how much slower Tess was walking.
Years had passed since their last meeting, and
Ella saw that time had not been so kind to her
friend. Tess grabbed the iron railing and was
determined to match her friend's ability as best
she could. Once up top, Ella led her over to two
empty seats. The short, intense trip exacted a
toll; they waited until her breathing got back
to normal. Ella took Tess's hands in hers. They
were warm and clammy. Tess's eyes filled with
tears. Her voice played out low and slowed like
a funeral dirge.

"I thought I had lost you, how did we let
this happen after all we had shared? We used

to talk to each other almost every day! Where have you been living...?"

Ella pulled herself back down from floating on the ceiling. Finding Tess seemed unreal yet undeniable. To retell the story of the last years, starting with the death of her husband and the move to the colony was not something she wanted to do in a quick rundown. They took turns sharing the vignettes, the mundane and drastic details. Overall, the answer was simple; they both suffered a loss when communication was chaotic and life very unpredictable. Ella knew she had gone blank for a while back then and cut off many people. It was not a black hole in her life, more like being hidden in a tunnel where you saw the light at the other end but didn't know when you would get there or if you cared. Everything had happened at once, loss, grief then more loss. All that time, Tess was only a few hours away. Tess let off a barrage of questions, "Are you still with the Institute study? Why did you agree to this trip? I am in their penalty box. They are going to 'fix' me whatever that means."

Ella grabbed on to her questions with a strange sense of relief to be finally sharing her questioning of the Institute's agenda and motives and what might lie ahead in the next two weeks. They compared quick notes on their wellness companions, making fun of the nurse Ratchet nature of their austere hyper-focused authority and their constant mantras on living longer practices.

"I am not sure," said Ella. "I am either having a nice break, and they will heap all sorts of praise upon me when I give more superior bio samples, or they will tell me I am going to live to a hundred. According to my friend, I am about to be sliced diced and distributed out as an ingredient for a genetic longevity tonic."

Tess gave off a nervous laugh and shook her head with a look of disbelief. "And I thought you were always the sensible one."

"But you were the one who talked me into this damned study so that we could grow old, old together!" Ella threw the barb with a strong hint of regret then slid into a softer tone.

"I think there is something to my friend's theories. How many people over the age of 80 do you know out in the community?"

Tess tilted her head back and then to the side, "To tell you the truth, I have known of a few older folks that packed a bag and did not come back. There was never an explanation, no goodbyes, they just keep releasing the empty housing."

Ella bit her lip. Then Tess added, "Maybe we should both be grateful we are still healthy enough to be worthy of all this scrutiny. I thought they were dropping me from the study as my health has taken a real dive in the last few months."

Ella pushed back, "Why would they ask you to travel all this way, and to what end? I thought when we joined this study it was to help further knowledge about people's health spans, not be the object of a mining expedition. I have been trying to read about the genomes and mitochondria."

"I know, said Tess, "neither of our parents lived long lives." but Ella stopped her there.

"Too much about the past, we have so little time to talk. The clock is ticking on this excursion. Your companion has probably already contacted Mattie to let her know I am also AWOL."

"Enough," said Tess, "I want to know what you are doing now. Do you still work? Do you have any relatives left? Have you been able to travel outside the state? I have been staring at the walls of my condo for the last five years going stir crazy, afraid to do much at all."

Ella stared off for a moment feeling guilty knowing she was debating even returning to the colony. They agreed on a plan to get more time on the layover without all the smothering from their keepers. "We will just show up at the same spot at the layover, and maybe they will go off together, and we can have some privacy. Text me when you are almost to the tower. We will see if they fall for this." Tess agreed.

Ella led her friend back to the bottom of the stairway and back to her seat. The train would be pulling into the New Charleston station soon. Back in her seat, she braced herself for the next stop, the whistle signal so shrill it rattled you to attention. She was still plotting how to steal a password, but that would have to wait until later. She wanted to let Riley know that she will not be meeting her as planned in New Charleston, but she was not returning her texts. Back in her seat, Mattie greeted her with a sour smile then extracted penance for having been out of her sight for forty minutes. She listened as Mattie went over what they were going to do every minute of the layover. Not my plan, Ella promised to herself.

CHAPTER 24

Riley shuffled down the aisle as the line formed to get off the train, no sign of Ella. Maybe the no texting thing was stupid; perhaps she should turn her phone back on. She almost jumped off the last step of the train to keep up with the press of everyone behind her. As she landed, the ache in her hips reminded her to take another pill. The local map seemed very basic. People were dispersing in so many different directions. She realized that for those who treated the whole train ride as a party road trip, this was familiar territory. Most of the repeat passengers ignored the perimeter of security vehicles and the helicopter overhead. It was as if they had parachuted into enemy territory, but there was a thick bubble of security agents protecting them scanning for potential trouble. If anyone strayed too far, their travel bracelet would help rein him or her back into safer territory. Some choose to stay on the train.

How was she supposed to know the layout of New Charlestown when she had never been to the original city by the sea? Climate sea rise had eaten away at the East coast in a fair and equal manner. Simply put, part of the former inland now existed as a coastline. The weather seemed somewhat neutral, almost indifferent, not too much wind or too much dampness. As she wrapped her second jacket over her shoulders, she looked around her. Who were most of these people, tourists or residents? If they were, she couldn't tell them from the train passengers. Pre-trip public service announcements advised everyone that part of this region was partitioned off as a different city-state area. Some of the original holdouts to the new social system lived beyond certain boundaries. All passengers had been warned to stay within the set zones for the tourist attractions and not go any deeper into the outlands. The live free or die clans were always ready to take what they could.

As she headed for the tower landmark, she passed unique little shops selling pricey craft items and some specialty foods. She guessed that old Charlestown was historical, charming but a classic tourist trap, not much here of interest for her. From the corner of her eye, she spotted the bell tower. She was to pass by it, and then turn left. She faced an odd-shaped pier high above the water level. Several giant porch swings stood facing what they called the new sea. A long line of people was already forming. She noticed a bronze plaque off to the side, but she did not bother to try to read it. An arm was sticking up, motioning for her to join him in line. Riley set her shoulders back and walked over to him as if he was her oldest friend. She heard some grumbles when she cut the line, but she didn't care.

As she slid in beside him, her skin prickled at the back of her neck. Everyone was shuffling forward as close to each other as possible. The train passengers knew their time was short and acted as if inches would make a difference. She wanted her usual boundaries, her safe space, but she would have to pass on that for a little while. Without even a hello, he launched again into a whole narration of the history of these swings. He explained how the Reconstructionist movement had the forethought to dismantle and move them as the sea rise encroached. She recognized a caustic remark bubbling up from her treasure trove of cynical material; something about did he ever work as a tour guide, but she stopped and paid attention. He gave the impression of being happy to explain what he knew about other efforts to save the coastal cities and their legacy landmarks. Riley surprised herself and chimed in.

"Yeah, seeing the Inner Harbor now gives me a real perspective, it could all be gone, but they saved what they could."

The line was orderly, the wait not that long. By their turn to share the swing, her prickly barbs had receded. Either this guy had great charm, or he was reading her well or both. By now, they had exchanged the war stories of their generation. Both had problems getting through school, finding little more than basic work on the other side and then having to relocate and start all over. They both were active in some of the major protests. Their politics were the default politics of their generation, fix it, fix it now and do not mess with us. They both confessed to still trying to make sense of their lives without any assurance of anything resembling a secure future. He had the physical scars to show for it. She recognized his uneven gait from a busted kneecap only partially repaired. He was making so much sense to her now.

As they edged closer to the front of the line, she noticed other couples and families cuddling up on the swing and taking their time to drift back and forth with the new ocean of New Charleston in their view. She tensed up again. What kind of moves would he put on her if at all? As they climbed on the swing, he directed her to sit sideways on the other end so that their feet touched in the middle as they faced each other. Okay, that works for me, she admitted to herself.

As the attendant pushed them off, he raised a finger to his lips.

"Listen to the sound of the swing."

She allowed the soles of her boots to line up with his. She focused on his closed eyelids and his fixed smile while her breathing quieted. The motion produced a cadence of squeaks and squawks that gradually softened in tone and tempo. It took a few minutes to hit a point when the sound disappeared, but the motion continued ever so slightly, a movable feast of meditation. This effort to blank out her mind and just be there was novel, something she had not attempted in a long time. Towards the end, she felt her eyelids close, reaching a moment of peace or surrender to trust. The attendant's clap brought her back to time and place. He sat there smiling at her and said, "I go by Grayson, who might you be?"

On the walk back to the train, they indulged in a full torrent of shared history. Both were still uncertain about the future even though they were more than halfway through their lives. In hearing the mixed bitterness of his tale, she recognized her own. These last few moments were disorienting and intoxicating at the same time as she shared truths about herself. It was a level of intimacy she rejected long ago. As they approached the line to get back on the train, Riley looked over at him strolling with his hands in his pockets, all of a sudden silent as a stone. He was putting the ball in her court, maybe waiting to see what she would say or do. There were a couple more stations/city stops, but the trip itself would be over by late afternoon tomorrow. In his silence, her defenses came back up. She admitted she didn't know what she wanted to happen. They were almost to the train steps when Grayson turned and asked, "Catch me at breakfast tomorrow, 4th car back?" His tone had will you please ring to it. His hard-core demeanor was softening. "Sure, that would be good," she shot back and then boarded the next car down.

This is what she needed, wanted, time to process, and decide what this meant to her if anything. Her intimacy meter registered on overload. Her usual levels of suspicion had been suspended. She could avoid him tomorrow, but she wanted to bring up her theory about the purging of older citizens. He might know more as he traveled all the time. Surely, Grayson would fit well in her search for the truth. She knew now he had the brooding soul of a fighter, not someone who would ever give up. What harm would it be to talk with him again? Research she says to herself, just research.

CHAPTER 25

The weather app had blasted out a positive cheery all clear for air quality, no masks necessary as they pulled in to New Charleston. As they stepped off the train, Ella sensed a change, was it the sky, the lightness of the wind or the crisp air she was breathing. It rested lighter, fresher as if something had been strained out of it. Past the station gate, she caught sight of trees. Were they real? Ella and Tess left the train separately, but both of them led their cohorts to the closest landmark just beyond the train station as planned. Then Tess feigned problems with walking and Ella offered to stay and sit with her while the two nursemaids marched off.

"Well that worked like a charm," Tess said as she tried in vain to make herself comfortable on the hard bench. "My joints hurt when I sit, or when I walk,"

Ella pulled a small inflatable pillow out of her bag, plumped it up, and pushed it between Tess's lower back and the hard bench. "Aw that is an improvement," sighed Tess rubbing her legs at the same time. For a while, they sat and took in the sight of the train passengers now local tourists sprinting about the little stalls that were near the station. There were fake ice cream treats and other snacks to be ransomed if you waited in line long enough. Ella noticed some security people well stationed at specific points and tried not to think about the possibilities of random attacks. She wanted to launch in her real feelings about the study and Riley's theories, but seeing her friend in such obvious discomfort made it easier to focus on Tess's view of the world. She listened as Tess talked of doing well until last year when the Institute introduced another supplement into her regimen. Ella remembered the buzz about it being the newest latest most exceptional way to add joint health to your years. At this point in Longevity science, they were trying to claim that no one should have to experience the creakiness of old age.

"They got me to agree to this trip because they are doing follow up for people who are having an adverse reaction. Age is age. If you keep trying to fight it, deny it, why would it not come back with a vengeance."

Ella laughed, "Yes, this fighting off aging is tiring in its own way." She recognized her friend's resignation to be passive about the whole experience. She could use more of Riley's rhetoric to stir Tess up. It would not take much. They both recognized potential for the predatory intent of the Institute; she would make matters worse by revealing her fears of shadowy departures without anything concrete to back it up. It was the bond between them. Ella knew she could say anything and Tess would not judge her.

Better right now to talk about what is real. They spun more tales about their current lives until the shrill whistle of the train called. Miss your train, and you were seriously out of luck. Mattie and her bookend hustled down the side of the pavement with more relaxed looks on their faces. Ella turned to Tess. "I would guess they know they had been outmaneuvered but are better for the whole experience."

"I hope you two had a good time," Mattie was the first to speak.

"Yes, we had a great time. We want to ask if we could trade off the sleeping berths for tonight so we can spend more time catching up." Ella asked, feeling bolder by the minute. Mattie shot a look at her coworker, and they put their heads together. Tess's keeper seemed much more inclined to do the switch. "Okay, but we will trade off again in the morning. We have details to go over with you both before we hit the Institute."

Ella swallowed her enthusiasm yet felt her whole body relax, she now had a new ally, even as Riley had somehow disappeared for now. There would be time to bring Tess up to date and maybe play with some more password combinations. With only one stop before the train arrived for the transfer to Lakeland, Ella knew she had to make her move. There was another stage in the final sign off to complete the trip or back out. She texted Riley again and hoped for an immediate response, but nothing came back.

Ella and Tess parted with a long hug and followed their companions back to the train. As they settled into the seats, Ella turned away from Mattie and fixed her sight out the window. Throughout the trip, she had watched the landscape change. Was that green grass or maybe just moss on rocks on the side of dead trees? The temperature was creeping up as the weather alerts came on again only to declare good news on this next section of the passage - sunny with a touch of medium humidity. She found herself drawn to everything passing by, more actual towns, and growhouse farms. Her head told her not to get too distracted; she needed to find out more about the Institute's plans for her before having to go behind locked doors. Mattie sat silent for once, wrapped up in her thoughts. Ella decided to invent another nap and let her head lean back against the headrest but kept Mattie in view.

Sure enough, once she was still, Mattie pulled out her tablet to record the shenanigans of the day or check-in. Ella counted keystrokes. The password consisted of nine letters, followed by four numbers. First Letter capped. The last four digits were the current year. She spotted enough to memorize some of the letters. There was an 'I' followed by an 'o,' another 'e' and 'o.' The other letters were from the mid-rows and harder to see. It amounted to more letters than she had before. She tried to close her eyes and start a mini sorting session of possible password combinations but as they pulled out a different siren sounded. An announcement, they would be passing through a microburst but no need to shelter in place. The train car rumbled, and the window shades descended, the train pushed forward through high winds, a drowning rain, and hail with no hesitation.

CHAPTER 26

Alvi opened her email, read Harold's note that he would be away for an extended visit. It could only be with the grandnephew. She let out a small yell, "Yes!" Now she had an opportunity to leave. First, Ella was off to her health study, and then Riley had a more extended work trip. It was like a bonus spring break. This was her chance. After spending time in Harold's unit the other night, she had relaxed her concerns about his mental state. Direct family time at his age was always a gift. The only other people in the colony were the several older couples who still managed to fend for themselves and the new younger couples.

Late last night, Maya finally responded, she had no contact from their parents. Alvi berated herself for letting them go without a more solid check-in schedule. She was going to track them down. She filled a backpack and researched her school options. There were class assignments, but she could work around them. Her pulse was racing now, balancing briefly between the worry that she would threaten her school status and the challenge to go against her mother's wishes. It was creating many ripples in her steady as you go status quo, but she had to face them. She remembered a quick mental exercise she learned in school and imagined approaching the scales of justice. Where would she put her finger on the scale? Staying was suffocating her. Going south to find her parents with or without her sister had to be the only answer. She would hand in her paper early, get a family emergency excuse for the next few classes, and hope to be back within a week. Her older sister had traveled south before. Being a journalist, she had special privileges to move around the country by air. That would be totally right in terms of timing if there were a safe weather flight window. Her mother talked very vaguely about where her aunt was going. Alvi and her sister knew of the gigantic retirement community where their aunt lived and worked for twenty years. They had never visited and did not have the new address, but they could start back at the old one.

Alvi put out a text for Maya to say she was calling. They needed to talk not just text. At last, the cell rang, and Maya answered.

"I have not been able to talk to mom or dad for over a week, have you heard from them?" Alvi heard the measured silence on the other end and recognized its familiarity. Her big sister was preparing to lecture her or soften the blow of bad news. Silence was always Maya's preamble as if she was waiting for an audience to gather.

"No, I have not heard from them. How is school going?"

"Do not try and change the subject. You know more than you are telling me, get off your journalist tight lip from sources bit and tell me what is going on."

Maya hung silent again, playing referee as to what to tell. Alvi knew it would not make a difference even if they were in the same room. She was being coddled. Her parents brought that to an art form when she was young. Now it felt like a betrayal.

Finally, she heard Maya sigh, "Okay. Okay, so Aunt Lena is not doing well. Mom voiced some concern about her situation down there and that Lena might make some rash decisions. If you have not heard from them, it is because they want privacy to deal with it and you have to respect that."

"Why, am I not a part of this family? I deal with decline all the time; remember it is part of my job. I am not the 5-year-old you had to keep in the house all day and away from everything media," bleated Alvi.

"Then you are mature enough to understand you have to trust mom with whatever plan she has made to help Aunt Lena. I am just finishing an assignment, but I am slated to go south in a few days. I have full travel privileges for my next assignment, and I can request to bring an aide along and we can fly instead of trying to get a train, we don't have time to wait. We could be there by the weekend and go to her old address at the community and work our way from there."

Alvi grabbed a chair, stunned that she had forced her sister's hand. This was a clear choice. Her oldest resident was off for a visit to his immediate CCR. She had options. At that moment, Alvi realized she had never flown before. She was tired of taking orders; it was time to be her own curator. Life needed to be met head on, even if death was waiting around the corner.

CHAPTER 27

Ella put her cell away and pulled the folds of the flimsy scarf up around her face. She realized the warmth of the sun had heated the thin fabric, and she savored its touch as it brushed against her cheek. It took her back ever so briefly to a better place, to that day she met little Edward and enjoyed what spring was accomplishing with the lone cherry tree. A small moment of homesickness swept over her. Talking with Tess had slowed the drip-drip of her negative thoughts. Even though they were on two different wellness levels, both of them were headed to the same place. Why did she have to see danger at every corner?

As the train finally started moving away from the last station stop, her eyes widened. A tall crabapple stood directly outside her window. It was a puzzle at first. Her sense of plants and their life cycles remained more acute than most, but she could not tell if the tree was dying off or regenerating. She scrutinized the tiny brownish red fruit and shriveled leaves that had met the chaotic season and survived. The sight was a mix of both stark death and radiant life as if clinging to existence was an ordinary state of affairs. Between the contorted branches, she strained to look even closer. In the nook of a larger branch rested a small bundle of fresh pieces of lint, cloth, and straw woven tight. Maybe it was an admirable start of a nest for an aspiring robin or even a small chickadee. As the train moved her out of range, she rested her head against the back of the seat. Well if the birds were acting as if there was a future, why couldn't she believe in change? You can build a life strand by strand. Her neck craned backward as the train picked up speed, no time to take a phone pic. She burned a copy in her brain. This was pure proof that life could go on and renew itself out there. Screw the worry, time to change the channel.

When Mattie returned from another restroom run, Ella pushed to drop the topic of health and find out how much her companion knew about climate restoration in the southern states. She turned out to be quite knowledgeable about the changing terrain and efforts to keep the sea rise contained.

"I make this trip an average of twice a month," she advised with her air of authority.

She explained that while crop growth was very regulated and deliberate, little by little wild plants were reappearing. The south still had warm temperatures most of the year. The main problem remained massive flooding storms. Some plants continued to adapt on their own even as horticulture specialists invented, spliced, and diced new plant species for the growhouses. "Wait until we get all the way to Orlando, they have spent a bunch of money to restore some of the environment there."

Ella immersed herself in as much information as Mattie gushed out. In true bureaucratic form, she painted a positive picture of what capitalized business of science and tech could accomplish working with a socialist norm-based government. Translation, citizens wanted a livable environment to survive, and big tech was making that happen to a limited extent. Nobody starved or was homeless for long once the money for the defense of a nation became funds for rebuilding after the climate assault on life and liberty. The government still needed the innovation of big business behind it all. Then, Mattie took another detour back to her data niche and went on about how people were living longer by renewing life with chromosomal transplants and gene implants for specific disorders, cloning basic body parts and 'genomic intervention' as she called it. Her theme seemed to be that life could go on and on if we all pitched in.

The reality that this woman was a total longevity nerd was clear to Ella. Everything she declared would be from her tech prone brain perspective. Ella would have to use her judgment to figure out what the Institute gained from mining all the samples she had given over the years and especially in the last six months. If all they were doing was prototyping her genetic lineage and lifestyle choices to make a longer stronger life for others, she was okay with that. However, Mattie took another curve back to talking about cellular senesce and pumping up telomeres for increased longevity. "That must be very difficult to quantify," said Ella.

Good grief, I am talking like her now.

She lapsed into her pretend listening/nodding mode again. Her mind needed to work on loftier thoughts. Why had it taken her all these years to realize that most of us die an inch at a time? Why not try to live a yard at a time?

Again, her only escape was to look out the window. The view had provided more signs of life in the past hours than years back home.

Ignoring Mattie's technobabble, she drew mental blinders down to concentrate on her thoughts. The answer clicked in as if her soul, brain, and body were all huddled on the same field at the same time, talking strategy ready to throw a long pass. Ella fathomed why she did not want to be a part of the Institute venture anymore. For the last ten years, she talked herself into believing that she could never live outside the colony. Her life would have to be a repetition of everything she had already done. Her little garden and few acquaintances would have to be enough, and for that, she should be grateful. This whole trip was a completely new tonic, meeting up with Tess again, and being among the spirit of so many people thinking good thoughts.

Others had spent years trying to relocate, readjust, and restart their former lives. Her friend Tess was losing steam. The idea of outliving so many friends was woeful. What good were all these extra years she was supposed to have if she didn't do something with them? She desperately wanted to sit down and talk this out with Riley. They would reach the Lakeland station tomorrow in the late afternoon. She wanted out from under the yoke of this study. By tonight, she would try to hack into Mattie's

tablet one more time. Whether she failed or
not to find anything, she was on her own. She
would rip up the contract and take her chances. Why give them credit for her graceful aging. She had been waiting to see her destiny
written in the clinical notes. Maybe it was time
she wrote her own.

CHAPTER 28

As Riley climbed the iron stairs, she debated again telling Lindy what had happened with the guy in New Charlestown, but then she would have to be honest about knowing what it all meant. For once, she was a crossroad with clear signs; ignore him or meet him for breakfast and find out more. Grayson's last words to her were, "I am also working on the boat you may be taking out of Tampa. I will find you." Walking and talking with Grayson, she was free to say anything from her most far-out theories, to share more about her past. He did not seem to judge her and was closer to a peer than anyone she has met in a long time. For once, she did not feel like the segment from an old children's program, one of these things is not like the other. She wanted to look harder into the mirror of his past and future ambitions.

As she slid into her seat, Lindy stopped her before she spoke.

"I'm not doing more than Tampa and will be going back as soon as we finish the work

at the pre-conference. I just got a notice. We
are in the top two groups for the full Denmark
trip already. That is too much of a trip for me.
I wanted to tell you first, but I will let them
know the first day of the conference."

Riley didn't bother to give any pretext of
being upset; this was exactly what she wanted.
It put another wrinkle in the plan but a good
smooth one that could lead to asking for a substitute and present Ella's coding background.
In another two weeks, they could be off to
Denmark on a boat or military transport. With
no contact since the lunch car yesterday, maybe she should turn on her cell. Their texts laid
out the drama in minimum characters:

    Ella: Sori for Chrstwn Much to tell
    Riley: yu can sub for L- to DenM!
    Ella: Good – get me out of this
    Riley: Stay on trn will find yu
    Ella: k – need to get my act together

Mattie marched off to the next sleeper car. Ella heard Tess swearing from across the aisle. After a few minutes, there was a light knock on the compartment door. Tess stuck her head in and whispered, "Guess what my keeper left in my room, her Institute tablet. You know how to work around these things much better than I."

She handed it over to Ella. They tried to both fit inside the compartment, but it was impossible.

"I have been practicing, and I have five new possible combinations from what I saw Mattie input on hers. What if it is a personal password, not the Institute password?"

"Well try it anyway. You have nothing to lose."

"Okay, you go back to your berth and try and get some rest. I will text you if I come up with anything."

Once the door snapped shut, Ella hoisted herself up and settled in the bunk, took out a reading light, and went to work. Even if she

ended up on her way to Denmark as Riley's
coder, she wanted to know what this genetic
fishing trip was all about. On the fifth attempt,
'Biogenomics 2039!' unlocked the device. First,
she searched for Tess's file. The files were all by
number not by name, but Tess had shared her
lifelong ID number and other security data. No
problem she was in! Ella decided to read only
the summary pages and one to two years back
notes. In the right margins was a block of information, a DFF score. The number space was
blank for Tess, To Be Determined. In tiny print
was the explanation, years, days of future wellness found past age 65 by evidence of a check-
box of DNA and other factors. So this was the
live long and well score she had heard rumors
about. Farther down, she saw lab pages that
were only partly decipherable to her. Testing
results were not going to be useful unless they
were flagged as out of normal range.

She rested on her elbow and turned towards
the tablet, resting on the wall of the small
space. Tess's last two summaries were brief. A
doctor argued that Tess's original records indi-
cated she should have succumbed to a family
incurable genetic disease over ten years ago,
yet she did not carry the gene. Reading on, it
pointed to trying some additional supplements.
The latest summary recommended the bigger

Florida study with emphasis on getting other family of origin DNA samples to confirm that Tess must have been adopted but unaware of her status. Then, to answer that, someone had entered a phrase about being an elder orphan with no living relatives to confirm this. Her adoptive parents had died of unnatural causes. The phrase, 'true natural longevity cannot be determined' was inserted in several sections. Then a warning, this information was not to be shared with the study participant.

Whoa, what am I going to do with this? Ella stared at the screen.

The only positive lead was an honest statement about trying to rectify the incorrect use of advanced supplements to bring her back to pre-morbid functioning. In other words, the Institute wanted to see if they could undo what they should never have done. The supplement had been tested further on a broader range of subjects and had the opposite effect of making cartilage solidify in 15% of those subjects. No wonder Tess moved as if rubber bands at her hips, knees, and ankles bound her. It was supposed to be a minor nuisance, not a life-limiting condition. She put the tablet up against the wall and propped a pillow over it. Her head started to drift down, but she shook herself awake. Tess may have already fallen asleep.

Ella had time to think about what to tell her before they met the keepers for breakfast. At least Tess was at no more risk than being in a standard medical trial. She could share two pieces of useful information to offset the message that her parents adopted her and never let her know. Time for a break, she tried to adjust the temperature and the flow of air pushing the buttons on the digital thermostat. It helped a little. Fumbling in her pocket, she found the extra squares of chocolate from lunch. First, she savored their sweet smell then the creamy, pungent taste. No rest now, she must get into her chart and find out what made her worthy of a home visit and the expense paid trip to medical wonderland. What is the mystery of why Ms. Ella is so age retro... a term she heard in the news a while ago?

She rolled back on her other side and brought the tablet up close beside her. The file came right up as she keyed in her ID number. An additional lock note sat on the last entry into her file that was still in draft form - No Unauthorized Entry. The previous full note had the date she submitted her agreement to come on this trip. She read down the column and went into Project Goals. Looking at the graphs that represented the comparisons to the stats of long-living subjects, it started to make sense to her. All this talk about the usual parameters was backed up by concrete evidence of genetic markers for longevity. The chart noted that she had no discernible current genetic markers, and yet her longevity mapping was set at 15 to 17 years younger than her chronological age. It all added up to a significant DFF number of days to live in a future that was still changing in waves.

There was something else, another chart about a special DNA factor but no parameters of hers matched the others on the chart. Why did they want to keep testing her? There was no simple answer. It was clear the Institute was still hoping to match her up with some magic Pandora's Box of particular DNA. How could one person's anatomy contain the answer to how everyone could beat the odds of normal aging? If she was not born with it, how did she acquire it?

Ella flipped over and put her head in the bedclothes to stifle a scream and block out her thoughts for a moment. She had wandered down a series of long corridors only to come to find a locked door. A post-it entry showed Mattie was still waiting on some newer biometrics from the last of Ella's bio samples. The note promised they would be available by their arrival at the Florida Institute. They were not giving up, one more bid to identify her intrinsic worth even before she got to main grounds of the Institute. Too late to sneak the tablet back into Tess's compartment; she would have to be up early. She would not have a chance to see the records again unless she pulled Mattie away from her tablet.

She set her alarm and turned over to face the compartment ceiling. The quilted padding made her think of a satin-lined coffin. This is what it must feel like to be buried alive even in this premium berth. A tightness in her chest was getting worse as if someone was wrapping a rope around her core and pulling slowly to choke the life out of her. She took a small keepsake from her bag and rubbed her fingers along its engraving while also massaging the left side of her neck. Her old doc had taught her this to stop a rapid heartbeat. A few more steady breaths... a few more gentle circles. She recited to herself this was nothing urgent. Each breath got deeper and longer, reminding her, she was in control and that she could push aside this blanket of fear.

A dozen years ago, she had endured the loss of her husband and niece. Within a year, she packed up and started a new life. Tasting such bitterness had made her more cautious as decisions have consequences. In her mind, she still reworked the series of events the night of her husband's death. The bullet that killed her husband was meant for someone else. Walking into the path of a drive-by shooting at that precise moment was a cruel piece of fate. The recreational drugs her niece had taken were tainted with minute traces of something deadlier. Sometimes destiny presented itself in inches and grams to take away what should be yours. Her deep well of grief taught her to move forward but also to not to count on good luck. She could now accept that there was no magic to survive in this world, only calculated choices to build your own happiness. If fate intervened, you were not responsible. Back then, direct action became a healthy alternative to smothering herself with dread.

Her choices were to lie awake all night and do a bunch of what-ifs. Weaving in Riley's back-stories of secret societies that looked for the ultimate life-extending cure would not help. Greed for money and power still ruled Riley's suspicious view of the world. Riley was right to warn her that the Institute only had her under a lens for what it could gain from her, not for her well-being. Nevertheless, they were running out of options to score some worthy new discoveries in all her lab work. If there wasn't any profitable magic bullet from her to duplicate, then none of this mattered. Going behind the walls of the place where giant people puppets used to walk around was not going to be a disaster. She smiled to herself. Maybe they should be looking in my mind!

She faced the sliver of light peeking around the edges of the stiff curtains. She bunched up the fake lavender scented pillows and let out a final sigh. There was a consolation prize for her piracy. The notes were not saying that her genetic material was highly marketable.

Tess's light across the aisle was out, and the shades were drawn. Tomorrow morning she would have plenty of time to put the tablet back. She adjusted the air vents again and curled up against the back of the compartment. Sleep was important, turning her mind off, a challenge. Ella made a pledge to herself. To believe fear keeps you safe is a fool's game. She would not run away. Instead, she planned to walk away from being a human lab experiment. Old age should carry with it an abundance of caution about some decisions, but for now, she relied on her version of what was real. She did not need Riley or the Institute to make it for her.

CHAPTER 30

Ella had woken up early, given Tess back the tablet and gone straight to the dining car. If Mattie chose to come looking for her, it did not matter. As Riley sat there at breakfast the next morning, Ella noticed something that looked like traces of excitement in her friend's usual solemn expression. Just around the corners of her mouth were little twitches as if she was trying to smother a smile or even a healthy grin.

"I apologize; I didn't mean to abandon you in New Charlestown..."

As Riley hesitated as if to say more, Ella took a breath and spilled it out. "Don't worry it all worked out. I ran into an old friend who is also in the study and we hoodwinked our keepers into letting us sit and talk alone. Bottom line, I figured out a password and hijacked an Institute tablet with the formal records on it and think I have nothing to worry about. They have been trying to make me a genetic trophy but can't find the key."

Riley shot back a puzzled look. "You are going to submit to the whole nine yards of more tests?"

"No, I am going to enjoy the rest of this trip and tell them to take me off their list when I get there. There is a final sign off point at which I still have the legal right to refuse any more testing. I may be able to get a ticket home. I read the fine print. But going back home might not be what I want to do."

Riley sat in silence. She had no hard-core ammunition to fire back at this practical decision. Her mind was already conjuring up the next negative scenario. What if the danger wasn't from the Institute but connected to just being in Florida?

Ella waited for a rebuttal to her suggestion, but her friend sat mute for once. She was finally winning this round but then quickly changed the subject.

"Fill me in, what have you... been up to?"

"Well for starters this is my second breakfast."

Ella recognized the expression on Riley's face and leaned in to share secrets. "I have to tell you something. I may not be going back at all either. I have the go head for the full Denmark trip." She hesitated. "And I met someone very interesting."

Ella's eyes opened wide and her face started to twist into a lopsided smile as she absorbed this dramatic change in course. She listened as her friend described in detail their initial meeting, their walk in New Charlestown, and their mental exercise on the giant swing.

Feeling playful, Ella said in a mock serious tone, "You have to follow that through, you always wanted to see Europe."

"With Lindy leaving before the boats sails, I could fit you in as my coding assistant for a few days at the conference if you really decide to bag out of the study. You know how crazy the temp coding hire situation is, you can still code in Quantum and Purge right?"

Ella shook her head, "It has been years since I coded full time, you would have to bring me up to speed so I could actually help you with the workload."

"I can't say for sure all the temps are going all the way to Denmark, but think of all the people you would meet if you did."

Ella dug her fork into the plate of fake scrambled eggs and tofu. The silence between them was softer and somehow very comfortable. Riley had taken the cue and they finished their meal without anything but simple pleasantries. Ella sensed they were both running scenarios through their minds, good, bad and indifferent with not much time to make final decisions.

CHAPTER 31

Maya gently nudged Alvi awake.

"We are in Tampa. I have to check in with the local bureau for my full assignment. They just let me know we will be on a cruise ship for part of it. Fancy that."

"I don't believe you slept through your first plane trip."

Alvi turned towards her sister as she watched her maneuver her bag from the overhead rack. Why did all of this seem like a dream? Why was she not back in the colony doing something practical and routine? Her manager approved the leave, but this was too much at once. Her heart rate kicked up, and her breathing became shallow. Out the window was the airport tarmac. Most of the planes had already taxied to a massive hanger built to withstand major storms. The other departing passengers seemed to have a layer of wealth wrapped around them in distinctive clothing and custom carry-ons. Her makeshift luggage screamed out; I do not know how to travel.

"Hey little sis, don't be so glum. I would think you would be glad to get away from the old folks' home."

Maya pulled her bag down the aisle. Alvi stepped in behind her. They emerged into a well of fierce sunshine; Alvi struggled to find the sunglasses Maya had given her. "Put on the visor I gave you. You do not want to look like a tourist, do you?" Maya teased.

Alvi shot back, "I thought you said everyone was a tourist here, that you can't live here year-round anymore." As she remembered, her aunt came north for the last ten tropical storm ridden Florida summers. Maya answered worthy of a journalist. "People still pick the best of what was is left of Florida. If you stay those four months a year, you live with hurricanes and the peak level heat - suffocating heat and the constant rebuilding. Not everyone is cut out for an annual endurance contest."

Alvi pulled up beside her sister and took longer strides. She was tired of being the tag-along kid. She had no idea where they were going, but she wanted to start this crazy search. Her parents were out there attending to her aunt's last days. They were not lost; she was. She wanted more answers. Why the secrecy? Why would you come for medical care to one of the most ravaged states? They were all the family that Aunt Lena had left. They had a right to be here. She wanted to be able to say goodbye and let her aunt know that she had already made a difference in her short life.

She looked around at the departing passengers and the people in the terminal. Nagging at her again was the reality that no one here looked like her elder residents at the colony. The idea that there must be some order or rationale for all this was still firmly ingrained in her. She had grown up to the mantra to follow the rules. What were the rules in this place? Maybe soon she would find out where many of her charges had gone.

CHAPTER 32

As she came back down the aisle, Mattie was planted in the aisle glaring at her. She frowned at her like a headmaster who was preparing to admonish their favorite prodigy. Ella mused about the unnecessary drama, all this for a few moments of peace at breakfast? Mattie stood with arms crossed in front of their seats and cranked up her tone to an even loftier level of official.

"I have something to tell you. We have to go where we can have some privacy."

Ella threw her shoulders back and took a moment to sort out feeling defensive and offensive at the same time. If attitude was everything right now, what right did this woman have to order her around? Her mind raced to the timing promised in the notes, what glorious news had come down from the labs. She made a gesture of after you, but Mattie let her pass as she pointed an icy finger towards the back cars. "We can have some privacy in the medical area." Ella sighed to herself; she had read and signed enough forms from the Institute to know she had some rights. Mattie continued behind her until they reached the medical car. Mattie talked briefly with one of the techs and then ushered Ella into a curtained off spot. On the short walk over, Ella thought about taking the initiative and challenging the whole idea of the study. It was not as if they could take back her high rating on biometrics. For the most part, she felt she had earned all of that.

The second they were behind the curtain, Mattie jumped right into a preamble about Ella's right and duties but then just laid it out.

"Your final bio samples came back, and your status has been downgraded as to what you can offer our study."

Ella took in a breath and waited for some kind of explanation.

"What exactly does that mean?"

"The consensus is that your DNA, blood plasma and other bio genomes markers do not contain any definable replicable biological element that is of primary interest to the Institute. Your unexplained natural resistance to aging has not been qualified in any of our current tests."

Ella felt the intended smack of the reprimand but just grinned back at her. Mattie pressed on with her declaration. Ella noticed the color draining out of Mattie's already ashen face. Maybe there would be repercussions for her for being matched with a non-producing subject. How competitive was this business?

"You have three options. First, come back with me, as I must return on tomorrow's train because your status does not warrant a personal escort. Two, you can go on the general studies portion of the Institute for any additional personal gain that might bring you and three, you can wait and use your original departure date at the end of the fourteen days with a hotel space paid for until then. You must advise me of your decision by the time we pull into the station."

Mattie then gazed off to the side as if Ella was supposed to disperse as an unwanted apparition. Ella stifled a laugh.

"So that is what all this has been for, so you guys can cash in on your prime subjects?"

Mattie paused as if she expected this and pumped up her tone even further but laid it out.

"Yes, this whole project is an investment in a healthy lifespan for all of us. Sometimes we see more potential in particular subjects. Your general health curve remains of interest to us, but we cannot find a way to duplicate it for others. Nevertheless, you have cooperated fully. If option three is your decision, we will make sure you return safely to your home."

Ella sensed this was a standard defensive maneuver on Mattie's part somewhere between anger and just dull disappointment when her subject was rejected from the A list. She decided to not press as to what duplication meant. She knew Mattie would dance around that in a pre-rehearsed manner. No way was she going to set foot on the Institute grounds.

"What about my friend Tess, is she staying for the whole venture?"

"Yes, she and her companion will be making the full trip to the Institute."

Mattie stiffened up as if she expected her to argue further about the manipulation of the whole venture. When Ella didn't protest, she just marched off for a late breakfast. Ella headed another car back to the exercise car. Yes, there was a treadmill open. She jumped on it and took a long hard walk and as she sorted through different emotions; anger, fear, and even giddiness. Once in rhythm walking at her usual pace, she let herself gaze out the window. What did she want at this moment? Maybe an old-style roadside billboard that explained all of this would appear out of nowhere. She wanted it to say Ella chooses to make a whole new life at age 65, and it works out tremendously.

Not, another older citizen disappears in the wilds of Florida never to be heard from again. She had been prepared to ditch the study, but now she had to face what this opportunity really meant. Then after a few moments, the real banner headline rose up in front of her. What was she going to do with the rest of her longer than usual life? She had to turn her A list status into something meaningful.

A trickle of anger was building, but at least part of the drama was answered. She was now officially a genomic outlier without a marketable value. The high-profile pressure from the Institute coupled with Riley's premonitions and her inherent fears had not been a pleasant combination. Like a slow walk through a deep forest, it meant now she had to emerge at an immediate fork in the road. She had a few hours to toy a little with choice two and three. Another option hung out there, to follow Riley on her work trip. She had to let her know right away to see if this crazy idea of her doing coding work was a possibility. She guessed that Tess's companion would have her on lockdown as they pulled into the station.

Ella finished on the treadmill and went back to her seat. Mattie was nowhere to be seen. She leaned over to capture more of the sun on her face and neck. Somewhere in the middle of this, she let her fears take a back seat. Being on this crazy party train headed to one of the most devastated parts of the country was a good thing. Everyone knew Florida had taken many mega-storms hits over the years and was always damp around the edges. Life there was still dodging destruction and defying weather patterns. In the high summer, it was more than an oven. It was a pressure cooker.

This time spent with Tess was like looking in a mirror. What she saw was her younger, more independent, and ambitious self before the decades of change. They had talked of plans made and plans diverted, but they always had their eye on the future back then. Tess was facing some real problems and was counting on still yet another medical intervention to put her back in self-sufficient mode. Maybe it was just the gift of being somewhere else with sunshine and not sinking in the isolation behind concrete walls. She texted Riley the news and saw an amusing string of playful emoji return almost instantly. New plan; meet her at the back of the train platform with her bags and they would be off to wherever Riley was supposed to be.

Her adventure surely was just beginning. She sat there stretched out on both seats until she saw Mattie filing back just before they pulled into the station. Again, she stood in the aisle with a dismissive look.

"Have you made a decision?

"Yes, I will skip the Institute but take the extended ticket and stay here for the two weeks."

A look of relief passed over Mattie. Maybe she would feel less like a failure if Ella's non-profitable body was not sitting next to her on the way back. Ella signed more e-forms, accepted some vouchers, and pulled her bags from under the seat. She refused to be dismissed like a naughty child who ruined the whole school trip. With her head held high, she turned to Mattie.

"I wish you all the best with your research work. You have given me a deeper perspective on many things." Mattie gave the slightest nod and turned away.

CHAPTER 33

Ella rolled her bag along the uneven stone walkway. A muffled thump bump sound followed her. The ground beneath her feet was a combination of smooth old stone and new concrete. A dozen artificial palm trees lined the path to the interior of the station, but she refrained from judging their appearance. The sight of the palms was a decent attempt to say glad you are here, please excuse us as we try to keep up appearances and reinvent life as we once knew it. Huge planters seemed to sprout at every corner crowned with complex plant arrangements that were also fake but held a proud riot of colors. There were perfect clones of the best of their extinct flora with richly veined broad leaves and bursts of reds and oranges and purples.

As she passed by, she extended her free arm to let her fingers brush against the bristly surface at the base of one tree to confirm the leathery delusion. The palms probably had steel rods up the center, and the fronds probably retracted during storms. The steamy air enveloped her in a gentle way, like having a movable cloak filled with pleasant traces of freshness. The ocean had come inland and was restrained by engineered structures, but the salt brine and the scent of marine life somehow still lingered in the air.

Riley was perched on a bench with her bag, her head down, reading off her tablet. As she approached, Ella saw her break into a strange smile. She pulled herself up and gave a silly salute.

"You did it. You lost them."

"No, more like they lost me. If the Institute can't find anything to capitalize on so it's goodbye, have a nice life." She could tell Riley had a snarky remark coming, but she stayed silent.

"Okay so you are a reject, that doesn't mean they are not exploiting others or would if they could. Aren't you worried about Tess? We need to keep in touch with her to find out more about what goes on in there."

"Tess is there to reverse something they did wrong. I will be in touch with her daily. She is smart enough to know if something is going badly. We will still be within helping distance."

Riley gave her another one of her; you are a fool to trust short speeches but ended with a pledge "If we have to get in there to help her, we will somehow."

Ella saw the determination in Riley's face and voice again. She could imagine a younger Riley with a bullhorn in her hand leading protestors into a confrontation.

"So here is the plan, I just got the okay for you to be my assistant for the first three days of the conference. After that, I will know if I am totally solid for the Denmark trip. You will have more time to decide and get your travel papers in order as a precaution."

Ella relaxed her grip on her bag. For once, Riley was thinking from her perspective.

"I have vouchers for a shuttle ride. It should be here any minute to take us down to Tampa with the rest of the coding crew."

"Wouldn't they notice that I am not Lindy?"

"No, not really, there is a mix of teams from separate regions. They deal with substitute temps all the time. No one ever really knows who is on the crew list, only if the work is complete and we meet our goals. As long as we keep ahead of the cyber threats, we could be trained orangutans if there were any of them left."

"Okay, I will go that far, but if I fail out, I am going to find my own way." Riley again gave her that strange new smile.

They piled into the van along with a dozen other company people. Ella once again found herself sitting in a seat going somewhere at the request of others. She craned her neck to see what she could from the full panel window. This New Florida was like an old postcard but somehow too perfect. She continued to guess that most of the landscaping was fake. One way or the other, it resembled pictures she had seen of tourist towns in Florida from years back, minus the barrier at the edge of the bay beyond the port entrance. The engineering came from copying the decades of effort and expertise from the Netherlands. A wall that flipped up and held back sea rise was the prime feature. Over the years, more and more of the climate defense money poured into rebuilding farther inland, as the coast became uninhabitable.

As they passed through the streets, they passed by an old-style boardwalk with lots of not so cheap souvenirs to prove you had made it to what was left of the sunshine state. It reminded her of the farmer's market in the Colony Center, a mixture of old boards and concrete reinforcement, trying to look authentic but braced for severe weather onslaughts. The van turned down the last lane of traffic, while still more vehicles came alongside them. This

was the closest to a traffic jam as she had experienced in a long time. It was a real sliding scale
of who could afford what level of transportation. Twisting in and out of traffic lanes, she
saw everything from a rickshaw pedaled jitney
to a long limo with solar panels.

Ella was looking the other way when she
heard a muffled cry next to her. Riley had
rolled down the window and was arching her
neck as they passed the line of cruise ships one
by one along the pier. The van stopped, and the
passengers jumped out to retrieve their bags.
As she turned, she could see Riley's face go
pale even as her eyes grew fierce. She choked
out the words in one breath.

"It is the ghost ship that I saw in the harbor
at home, loading the elders."

The calm feelings Ella had gathered in just
these few blocks escaped like air out of a bal-
loon. Once again, she needed to brace herself
against what was coming next.

"How can you be sure?"

Riley pulled out her cell and punched up a
picture from her gallery. "You know I am no
good with names. I took a picture that day. It's
the Klotho II."

Ella looked over at her friend and then to
the other passengers leaving the van and ca-
sually moving towards the ramp. She grabbed

her bag and followed them. Riley was following her still in a daze.

"So we are not being ushered to the back
door and into a secret passage," Ella quipped.

Riley kept looking over her shoulder to the
rear end of the ship scanning for evidence of
guards or orderlies. She was staring at the long
line of tech people with their luggage. Some
were scanning their devices as they waited to
go through the check-in process. Others were
families huddled together with their multiple
bags. In addition, of course, the lovebirds were
still with them.

Ella felt her flash of anxiety fade. Okay,
she was undoubtedly the oldest person in the
group, but no one was coming to retrieve her.
This was mostly the same mix of humanity as
on the train. It did not feel wrong at all -it felt
right- it was just another step toward her new
adventure whatever that was going to be.

PART THREE

THE GHOST SHIP

Harold stared at his bare toes peeking out from the silver woven blanket at the bottom of the bed. The attendants kept coming by and putting his slippers back on, each time with a sweet smile and a caution about body core temperatures. They were expertly reading every vital sign as body thermometer reading to death and demise. He did not care; he wanted to be out on deck as much as possible. In the last week, he had discovered beauty and power in one place as they made the passage down the eastern coast. The feel of the massive boat cutting through the silent power of the ocean waves was magical to him. In that time, he had become a new devotee, worshiping even the smallest view out to the ocean. Here in front of him occurred a majestic force he never took the time to witness before. The irony wasn't lost on him. He signed up and came on this trip to die, but now was firmly in awe of the forces of nature. Storms provided some rocky periods down below, but they all had enough Dramamine in their systems to make the passage. Every minute of this outside time, he embraced as a small treasure. The attendants would be coming soon to move him again. During the passage, the sound of the ocean spray against the side of the boat was faint, but he strained to make a melody out of it. He detected an undeniable tempo that he took back to his room to help lull himself off to sleep while remembering his music without the headphones.

Tears sat at the back of his eyes now. He had found a setting where he could gain a different perspective. His well-ordered life would decrescendo into a well-ordered death. His mind pushed forward, remembering the contract. There were so many different attendants. Even with the large nametags, he couldn't remember their names. When his appetite had left him several days ago, as he quietly refused most of his light meals, they did not press it.

After he contacted the Society, everything fell into place. He completed a brief People Time session with a very professional looking representative. They sent someone out to take some test samples for the Predictive Death Algorithm. It took a few days, but the same person came back with a second representative, and they explained his estimated time of survival considering his particular cardiac condition. With congestive heart failure, it was like watching a graph take a slow, low dance out the door. They were very gentle about it and practiced in their approach and completeness. He had maybe two to three weeks left. Harold couldn't help but think what a strange business to be in, granting people's last wishes to be able to know the circumstances of your death. For him, there was no desire to bargain for an extra-inning. If he wanted a wisp of more time, he could enlist some additional medical interventions. That would not be the fitting way to end a composition.

He would have liked them to use a more poetic approach, maybe bring a huge hourglass and flip it to start the grains of sand flowing. Instead, it was like a multiple-choice test. They just added up the facts and told him approximately how much time you have left, here are your choices, a, b and c. Forty years ago, doctors gave you one to two years to live if you agreed to the torture of chemo treatment. If you deferred, you got six months to let cancer eat away at you. He was grateful that he dodged that bullet which felled friends and family members at an earlier time. Now all he wanted to do was look back on how much he had lived, and be alert for what little was before him.

A quiet air of victory combined with the taste of sea air. They were at a dock again, and the big motion had ceased for now. He was content with the choice, a scenic trip, and then enough attention to feather his exit. The Klotho Society engaged a cast of characters on the ship to usher you along, from special nurses with the latest pain medication, and ministers if you were so inclined. Everyday parts of his body were succumbing to a strange numbness. He did not think it would be like this. No massive heart attack or stroke for him, it seemed. He was ebbing out of life like a stream that disappeared into a slow trickle.

His audio files were still with him, but his hearing had deteriorated so fast that listening to them became an out of body experience. If this constituted his life passing before his eyes, he was finally grading his own low-key self-centered performance. He had read once that death was never tidy but that it could be noble. In the grand sum of things, he realized how little impact he had made on the world. The simplicity of his life did not offend him. Maybe sometimes, you want no more than to coast through it and not make waves. Harold imagined the reaction of Colin when they send part of his liquefied remains back with an explanation and his final note. That thought gave him some satisfaction. The last of his financial re-sources would be a booster shot for the young growing family. He found no regret in his re-fusal to have children; he knew he was too self-ish to parent. Better to leave no offspring than estranged ones.

In total, he had left a faint trace to improve the world, nothing beyond the realm of a strict choral master. Maybe you add it all up, and if you did nothing evil, you would slip away into the void of non-being. His only legacy might be the few tears that Colin might shed. He never believed in the promise of an afterlife, and he never asked for one. At least his will would pass on something more than an apart-ment unit to clear out. He left several notes of thanks to Colin tucked in his books at the unit. They could well end up in someone else hands, who was to know. The attendant was coming now to bring him back down to his room on the other deck, no more outside time today un-til later. It was time for a gentle sponge bath and a medication check. If the weather permit-ted, he could hope for watching another sunset on a not so cloudy day.

CHAPTER 35

Ella sprung up from the cramped desk in the cabin and spun around. There was no porthole window in the cabin. The artificial light and the gray, silver décor made the room feel like a designer shoebox. With the boat still in the harbor, she was not worried about seasickness. For now, she felt queasy only over the task in front of her. She had completed pages of code revisions. Riley turned out to be a better tutor than she would have expected, but the wheels were turning slowly and so much had changed in the programming world. She finished the last of work Riley left and checked the inbox. Empty. She needed to get away from it for a while. This work/sleep cubicle on the ocean offered few distractions, no screen blasting out the all-true news and only a shaky connection and expensive access to her audio/video playlist.

Riley was out investigating the other decks. When no one from the Institute hijacked them getting on the boat, she had made the mistake of joking about it. Riley reminded her elders were still disappearing at a rapid rate without any explanation. Riley was Riley. She was still fixated on her death ship theories. There was an enemy out there, and she needed to vanquish it.

Ella decided to back off now that they were safe on the ship in their cabin. Ella tried to talk herself into accepting a simple reason for the gurneys she saw back in their homeport. Older people may need assistance going on a cruise, but gurneys, why not wheelchairs? Maybe Riley would come back from her walk around and focus on the decisions in hand. If there was no threat on the ship, they could calmly talk about all the options in front of them. They had to consider the fact that there was no final guarantee they would pick Riley for Denmark. She kept hailing it as a new beginning if they could emigrate with their skill sets. Riley was fixated on being on the A team for Denmark, but Ella understood there were too many ifs in that plan. Ella picked up the open return travel ticket and the hotel voucher for the next two weeks. This opportunity was real; this was the actual raffle for her future.

She closed the work laptop with a slight bang. Enough of this mirrored tomb, she needed air and light and color in front of her eyes.

She searched until she found her sister's embroidered shirt. Putting it on without an eco-jacket felt right. The cabin mini weather monitor declared seventy-five degrees and only partly cloudy. Sitting here in the harbor, in this massive ship, she had the same feeling of security that she had at the colony. Maybe it did not take concrete reinforced walls and security patrols to keep you safe. Perhaps it was being in the company of so many others trying to live their lives without fear. She felt more alive and comfortable here than anywhere else she had been in many years. Her head and her heart started pulling in two different directions. The Institute had released their tight grip on her. Her health and welfare were her responsibility. Maybe this nervous flitter and the thump/thud beating of her heart didn't translate into fear but the fresh excitement of having choices to make.

She could still stay one night and get right back on the next train north in the morning and avoid Mattie the whole way. She could spend a week or so and discover what Florida was all about then head back to her tiny world. Her coding skills were not as rusty as she thought, but Riley would do well to find a more seasoned work partner. All these thoughts clumped up inside her, but the feeling was worth the flip-flops going on in the pit of her stomach. She had no anchor here like in her little community with her well-worn path down and back to the only thing in town. Ella made her way out to the nearest deck at a spot where she could see the expanse of the horizon. The ocean salt brine mixed with other smells. She feasted on the sight and the scent of the colorful regrowth on the farther shore of reclaimed land. This was another vantage point to the view and her life. She had better get moving.

She found her way back into the narrow corridor to the elevator bays. Everyone she passed seemed to be smiling with open faces. Like the train, the passengers were happy with this rare treat to be out of the yoke of their everyday lives. She stared at the schematic of the ship. There was much to learn with this system of stairs and elevators and decks - so many floors. The center space of the atrium looked like it could swallow all of the walkways. With so much human traffic, she guessed the high meshed covered railings were there as a safety precaution to keep children or adults from flying down to their deaths. The old brass stair balusters wore patches of semi-shiny spots from the passing of thousands of hands. The carpet drab in color and texture looked out of place with the elaborate old crystal fixtures and ornate mirrors. For the vast amount of traffic that passed over, it was a practical choice. Full Pharma had solved the norovirus situation with immunizations, but there were still dispensers for hand sanitizing. She examined a very fine fake plant when her cell buzzed again, Riley texting - they had to be in the theater/conference room in twenty minutes.

CHAPTER 36

Maya stared at her cell and drew back with a grunt. "I have been reassigned." Alvi was piling their bags on a hotel cart. She turned towards her sister and put her hands out in a gesture.

"I thought you were used to this. You are always talking about being pulled from one info storm into another."

"Well, we can't go to Aunt Lena's old retirement community today. I have to report to Tampa first ...to a press gaggle on a ship."

"Maybe I better go on my own."

Maya glared back at her, "No, we stick together. It will not take long, it is just a two-hour heads-up meeting, and they know I am in range. I have no choice."

Alvi resisted a smart remark about Maya being at the mercy of her editors. She was not jealous of this part of her sister's life. Maya had a broader view of what was going on. She could give you a historical, geopolitical perspective in 300 words or less of any situation in the world at any time. She lived at a dizzying pace following what still needs to be investigated and exposed. The change was still happening, and it had to be followed and documented. Alvi knew that her sister's reporting could help make the right kind of change, and she was always ready to give her 110 percent. She gave her sister credit for that.

Her pause had given Maya time to catch her breath and think. The battering back and forth always took a toll on them.

"Meanwhile I can query Aunt Lena's old community under my information rights as a journalist and see if there is any forwarding info. I should have done that before we left."

"You mean a last known address?"

"No, that is ridiculous, so many people have migrated, moved, been transitioned, almost everyone has a few addresses. Her old community once had over 50,000 residents now it is just a trace of what it was. We tried to do a story on it before, but it was very murky as to what happened."

Alvi remembered something in her lectures about these larger communities of older people. They were almost obsolete.

"No, but I can ask about any financial resources left and if they have a link. I will make something up. It is the best way to trace people anymore is where they get their income checks. This is so low level no one will bother to question my press access."

"Mom did mention something about taking over the financial power of attorney for Aunt Lena."

Maya stopped texting for a moment. "Why did I not know that?"

"Because you spend your life flitting from place to place and we can never have more than a 10-minute conversation with you."

This time Maya turned away, even though Alvi saw a snarky remark forming. She watched the look on her sister's face change to one of both guilt and defeat. Alvi stepped ahead with the baggage, smiling to herself. For once, she had nailed her sister's attitude to the wall.

CHAPTER 37

Ella entered the theater meeting hall. Having never been on a cruise, she could only imagine all the glitter and sparkle, laughter, and applause that once filled the cavernous space. Riley motioned Ella to the seat beside her.

"I thought I said try to blend in." She glanced at Ella's colorful shirt and shook her head. "Just act like you belong here, there are other senior programmers here, and nobody will know, you could have written the textbook."

Ella opened her laptop and tried to look industrious. Her seat was a distraction, the velvet worn thin, but still luxuriously padded, it rotated forward, back, and swiveled left and right. She couldn't remember ever being in a theater with such plush comfortable seating. She leaned towards Riley and asked as quietly as she could, "So, what is on the agenda?" One side of the vaulted room filled up in just a few more minutes.

"Hell if I know," said Riley. "I am just waiting for my marching orders."

After the first two speakers had finished, Ella fully understood for the first time what Riley did for a living besides act as a courier. The project leader was pressing everyone to work harder as there had been a breach in the veracity software. The Communication Authority that encapsulated all news feeds and filtered out falsehoods had found a new threat. Over the last ten years, they had refined the whole system to make it less and less cumbersome, but there were always new malware worms trying to get into the system. Proprietary information dissemination had moved beyond its art and science stage. Most citizens, especially the younger segment of the population had graduated to be their own honorable judges of the truth, but most citizens wanted that simple ribbon of and all of this is true to keep dancing along at the bottom of their screens.

The news was not being subverted with false leads and algorithm gangs of foul bots, but the AOTT banner and WANT had both been scrubbed. The blowback had been immediate. A sizable portion of the population was not trusting anything, even the weather feeds and storm warnings. The company's CEO decided to speed up the Denmark trip to do a full reboot on the master servers. The coders who were making the whole trip would be notified by 6 AM tomorrow. By the next day, they would be on military transport and the rest sent home. The rumblings in the crowd seemed very mixed; many had not seen this as a full ticket ride anyway. Riley took a minute to compose herself then whispered to Ella,

"I am sorry to do this to you, but you have to decide tonight. If I am picked, I will be gone within 24 hours."

CHAPTER 38

They rolled their bags into the small hotel. Alvi watched as her sister maneuvered around the last-minute change in reservations with the desk clerk. Maya had mastered dealing with rapidly moving job assignments and arrangements. On the way to their assigned room, Alvi noticed a dozen other people taking possession of their ten by ten-sized rooms.

"They have been doing this in Japan for decades," Maya said as she unlocked the door. "They call them suitcase hotels; you sleep in a fold-up bed and have a petite bathroom and a small working surface."

"I get the lower bunk," as Maya pointed to a handle on the wall.

"So what else is new?" Alvi pulled the padded platform out into the tiny area of the room. She straightened out the folded mattress and started to climb up into her space. Her cell rang in her pocket with her mother's ringtone. She rolled over quickly and almost fell back off the bunk.

"Mom, what is going on? Maya and I are here in Florida."

A long silence sat on the other end, then muffled sounds, as her mother talked to their dad, then more mumbling.

"No, talk to me, hello, where are you?

Her mother fired back, "Why did you do this? What about school and your job? Put Maya on the phone."

"No, you talk to me. What you are hiding?" Alvi stopped as she heard herself yelling at her mother.

Another floating piece of silence hung in the air. "Well, I guess it is time to tell you, Aunt Lena is very near death, and we are here to be with her at the end. We did not want to involve you as that is her wish."

With the volume up, she did not have to repeat anything. They sat together on the lower bunk, and Alvi handed the cell to her sister and let her head sink into her cupped hands. She dangled in between pushing herself to be strong and the pull to let all her sorrow drain out.

Maya started talking in their native Kurdish. Alvi couldn't follow it very well. Her Syrian mother had decided at an early age to assimilate her second child totally into American culture. She caught something about the Clo...tho, a ship that was all she understood. She grabbed the cell back from her sister. Alvi pulled together a direct order to her mother in a calm voice.

"Tell us where you are - right now."

CHAPTER 39

As the meeting in the theater wrapped up, Ella faced an even tighter time clock to make a choice. She crossed out going with the A team to Denmark. That was Riley's fantasy. Starting over at her age in this crazy world did not seem so crazy anymore but not in a foreign country. She joked to herself. It is not that much of a big deal. I have to hurl myself into the future and find my own path. Going back sank to the bottom of her unwritten list.

She rode the elevator down to the lower deck. Once in the cabin, she tossed the company laptop on Riley's bed. Her final assignment was complete and logged in. She sorted through what clothes she had in her bag. An old seed catalog dropped onto the floor. She laughed, picked it up, and ran her fingers over the worn corners like a worry bead. Sometimes to fall asleep, she paged through the visual history of what you used to be able to grow in your garden, sorting through perennials, annuals, bulbs, and shrubs. At her old house, each spring she would pick a striking touch of color to nurture through the quixotic temperatures of spring through wicked wet summers. Past history, now she must focus on her very limited no frills future.

At least one full trip around the ship would clear her head. Back out to the corridor, she met a mix of the IT people and regular passengers who were lining up for early supper. Dinner would have to wait. She headed back out to the nearest deck that faced the ocean. Ella rewound her memory tapes of the well-paced pristine commercials for various resort vacations and wondered if the ocean water ever was that startling in their blue and greens. The water surface looked more like a lake on a gray day. Maybe this is what it looked like even before the pollution, before the desalination projects. She had read that many of the sustaining elements were still there but on a more minute scale. Algae and plankton had adapted somewhat along with the smallest marine life. The giant whales of literature and children's books and documentaries were echoes of the past.

Right now, the sky, clouds, and ocean blended into a blue gray haze at the horizon like one giant canvas waiting for some meaningful strokes to make it real. If there were a sunset tonight, it would be subtle and unassuming.

This was now a matter of fact life, you accepted what remained and championed its cause, or you lived down in a well of constant remorse. Preservationists had worked for the last decade to seed the ocean with new life. Ella was still adjusting to the briny smell. Maybe salinization plants put ions in the air. If she didn't even trust all her senses right now, how was she supposed to make a major decision? She could be swayed by being this close to all this renewed nature even if part of it was stagecraft. The longer she stood there, the clearer it was that the ocean was not handing out any solutions.

She pushed back from the railing and calculated all the stairs up, deck by deck. Walking always cleared her mind. Pacing up and back of this extended side deck was not cutting it. She wanted to scale up the side of this fortress to the top of the ship. Up one more deck at the top of the railing, she glanced both ways. Many of the same amorous couples from the train were out on the deck chairs. Here she certainly was the invisible older woman. They would ignore her doing handstands. She set to walking with her same assuredness that she felt in the colony. An air of authority never hurt in a situation like this. She didn't know what was off limits, but she wanted to keep heading up. She was trying to open up her world, and the more she could see the better. Being Riley's tag along, she was close to being a stowaway except for Lindy's substitute ID badge. It was time to take command of her mini journey here before she made some big decisions. Mixing and mingling with as many different types of passengers gave her more energy.

Each deck seemed to have a character of its own. The next two held more young lovers on the fertility clinic sponsored cruise. The couples lounged dressed in their best old cruise wear, like a colorful flock of birds chirping and attending to each other. The day's emerging partial sunshine had lured them out of the privacy of their cabins. Ella watched as couples responded to messages on their cells and attendants ushered them off to clinic visits or prompts to go make a baby. It had the odd mix of a sports event and a scientific conference complete with cheers of encouragement from the crowd. Riley had shared the tales from her younger coworkers. It demanded sustained effort to get the timing and the extra hormones just right. Ella half expected to see some sort of scoreboard up on the side of the deck.

Another deck held a smattering of the conference people out of their coding cabins trying to act as if they knew what to do with themselves away from a screen. The IT people were unremarkable, uniformed in their pale blandness and quiet voices. They could be anywhere and still look like the sun never touched them. She hiked up three more decks from front to back of the ship on both sides. This ship had only two decks of state-to-state migrants looking tired but hopeful. Families huddled together and stayed vigilant about their children and belongings. She heard hushed talk of destinations and plans.

The next deck up was almost empty so she could walk right along the railing and take another long look out to the ocean. Her heartbeat slid into a good rhythm spreading a sense of composure the longer she walked. This was the soothing point during her treadmill routine when she got a soft kick down in her breathing, her pulse evened out, and her mind cleared. What she truly wanted was an unobstructed view of her future. Up another two decks, she came around the next corner. An oversized curtain blocked off the rest of her path. Yards and yards of luxurious fabric made a ten-foot wall that could be breached with the simple swipe of her arm. She turned and looked behind her. No one else was in sight. The ship had the standard storm adaptations where vulnerable parts retracted and were sheltered in place against big winds. This curtain must be for privacy; otherwise, this mountain of cloth made no sense. A sign screaming Authorized Personnel Only was to her left, but she leaned in over the roped-off barrier. She moved even closer yearning to touch the folds of the fabric. Tiny silver emblems or logos were woven every few inches in the fabric. Her fingers ran over the cloth and stroked the raised silver bumps. This was new custom work, not a relic from an old theater. Tiny silver silkworms or small scissors? She stopped trying to make sense of the symbols and just admired the beauty and elegance of the design.

Behind her, the sun was hanging lower in a now azure sky. She was supposed to meet Riley down on their deck. She noted the deck number and began to turn when she heard music from behind the curtain. Maybe there was a first-class section after all, and the elites were celebrating back there. It only took her a moment to decide this next step - time to crash the party.

CHAPTER 40

Harold spotted the attendant coming with someone in an upright chair. "Oh no, here we go again," he muttered to himself. "Happy to share the view of the ocean?" he caught the sweet melodic tone of the attendant. He could refuse and burrow deeper under his blanket throw. Talking to others left him more exhausted, but the request had such a correct ring to it. We are all in the same boat here he chuckled to himself. He looked over at the small figure in the special wheelchair, a man maybe in his late fifties. Gnawed at by years of some disease or other, the fellow seemed to be enjoying being on deck as much as he was. Being outside was a treat even while the ship sat in the harbor. He may have spent many days inside a medical ward before coming here. The vastness of the sky belonged to everyone to enjoy. Harold turned his head a bit further and noticed a slight smile emerge under the big hat and sunglasses. No one bothered to enumerate his or her illnesses or medications on this deck. These passengers were way beyond that old people's pastime of counting doctors' visits, diagnoses, and pills. Life was still hovering over both of them even as death was out there drawing them nearer.

A voice came out of the man's throat clawing up out of a cave, rasping for air. "I wish I had traveled more. Never knew the power of all this."

Harold nodded. He balked at the injustice. This man was too damn young to be on a final journey. At least the fellow had a sense of peace about him.

"I hear they are setting sail in a day or two. This is an interesting schedule. They keep you guessing," said the tiny figure.

Harold replied, "It is better that way, it lets you know you are along for the ride, however long or short it may be."

After an attendant wheeled away his deck companion, Harold grasped at his regained solitude. Out here with the mild wind on the deck, but tucked in by the neatly arranged blankets, he felt like an envelope ready to slip under a door. Alone again, he could only ruminate on the thin substance of his life. Maybe he was waiting for some revelation that would add up to more than the sum of the simple parts of his life. People always clung to using that expression about passing away. In his mind, that meant you had to accept that you were at one location and that you would end up in another. He did not think he would warrant a hell if there were one, nor earn a place in someone else's idea of heaven. He had never been a war hero pulled from the ocean after a bombing mission, nor had he cheated and robbed others of their lives or liberty. Instead, he was ready just to stop being. A proper piece of music did that whether it ended on a loud crescendo or a soft fading sound.

CHAPTER 41

Riley shut off her tablet and got up from the chair, her lack of soreness a welcome surprise. It was like expecting a ghost that did not appear. The longer she sat in one place, the more painful it usually was to stretch out and move. Ella had given her two boxes of pain patches the night before. They were the last of the same experimental joint pain supplements that failed her friend Tess. She slapped several on her hips and knees that morning. Riley appreciated the gesture for her to share unauthorized property from the Institute, but she was not hopeful. Now hours later, the patches were still spreading a penetrating, soothing warmth. It was a definite improvement over her basic pain meds. She extended her legs and flexed her knees without the feel of grinding joints. Testing her limits, she did a deep knee bend and some other stretches. It was as if someone released bands off her wrists, knees, and ankles so she could move. She read the discarded package sleeve. A warning to avoid certain brands of protein bars with XYZ ingredients because of adverse allergic reactions. No list of active ingredients for the patches, just - Property of the Longevity Institute /Designated Consumer Use Only label.

Her brain said this must be a fluke. How long would the usual aches and stiffness stay away? Was there a downside to using these patches? Riley needed to let her usual skepticism run the gauntlet. Things never really turned out for her; it was some unwritten rule of her shaky karma, she had lived too long in her unique Riley universe cursed by timing and fate. She sent Ella a text. They needed to complete more of the prep work before late dining. Even though she was still on call for the long trip as of tomorrow morning, she had to finish the last of the protocols. Only so many hours remained.

The walls of the tiny cabin pressed in on her. Riley now had two reasons to get moving, or maybe three. Grayson was somewhere on this boat. He was not in the dining hall, and she didn't think he was part of the sailing staff. If he was part of the mechanical crew below the first deck, she was prohibited from that space. He said he would find her, so she had better get out there. She had gone over their talks in her head several times now. Their pasts had not intertwined to be in the same place at the same time but had been parallel as weary protest warriors. Both of them had old legal entanglements that they had evaded successfully. Europe together was brewing in her head like a well-written ending.

She did a quick read of the deck directory. They had changed some of the original names for the atrium and theater areas as they now served more as meeting and conference rooms. The old luxury liner had evolved into a floating conference center with a transition migrant hotel and a full fertility clinic. The younger couples were an obvious recent addition. Lindy had taken the sperm donor route without a life partner to launch herself into motherhood. She had shared anecdotes of her friends who had gone on this cruise with their husbands or partners to micromanage the fertility process and come back pregnant. It was like winning the baby lottery if the ovulation cycles lined up with good ocean weather. Riley guessed Deck 5 was where that magic happened. Deck 6 held a large gym/wellness center along with general health services. Everything on the boat seemed to encourage health, wellness, and community, so her death ship theories were again rattling around in an empty space. The ship map did not declare an area "go here" for disposing of seniors.

On the old luxury liners, the higher up your cabin, the more expensive the price tag. Two hundred thousand tons of cruise ship adapted well over time into a large community center with multipurpose uses. As far as she could tell, the other boats at the dock spent most of their time in port. Then she noticed a small blank area at the very top of the graphic. The words No Access were stamped in small red letters. She expected that to be on the lower level for the ship's boiler and mechanical rooms and the crew quarters. So up top was where you were not supposed to go, of course, she would start there.

CHAPTER 42

Maya had answered her cell for work and walked out to the hallway over twenty minutes ago. Alvi couldn't move around in the tiny room without wanting to put her foot through the flimsy walls. She packed and unpacked her bag, trying to remember what she had brought on this instant trip. There was no doubt that Maya would adhere to a work first rule; it had been her proven passport in the world of journalism. It riled her that Maya would rather have a stranger in the hallway overhear the conversation than her sister. She had put Alvi off by saying, "What you do not know can't hurt you."

If she was supposed to be the video/audio assistant as part of her airfare, she couldn't be subject blind. Maybe her sister's assignment kept changing, or she was trying to maneuver the logistics of finding her aunt. Alvi knew she was out of her domain. At the Colony, she could report in and ask for guidance. Instead, this was turning into a deeply personal family matter. The unease of not knowing what she should be doing at this very moment was growing into a heavy feeling in the pit of her stomach. The struggle between respecting her aunt and her mother's wishes and being pushed aside by Maya twisted her back into bad thoughts. She blamed herself for passing up opportunities over the last two years to keep more in touch. Aunt Lena had always lavished attention on her and her sister even during some of the very chaotic times. She dredged up the recall of days of teasing and name-calling in school. Her mixed heritage unnerved people more back then because they could not readily put her in a category. Lena always called her a special princess and promised her the world would learn to respect her, but first, she had to respect herself.

The door swung open. Maya stomped over, shoved Alvi sideways on the lower bunk, and threw herself back with cell still in her hand.

"I do not like this at all. This is all adding up wrong."

Alvi looked at her and waited for more. Silence. The look on Maya's face was a mix of surprise and anger. She was getting ready to fight back against a surprise enemy. Alvi bounced up and stood with her arms crossed, staring down at her sister.

"So what is the deal?"

"It seems our mother is involved in the same grateful death conspiracy I am supposed to be investigating." For a split second, Alvi let the room start to spin around her, but punched her emotions back in place.

"You have about ten seconds to start explaining what you just said before I go ballistic."

Maya pulled out her tablet. "It is time for a serious reality check. I need your truth radar on this one. You had classes in gerontech, right?" Alvi never thought it would come to this; she had information, and Maya did not. "What do you know about AI and death prediction algorithms?"

Alvi stepped back and pulled her hair, twirling a few strands around her fingers. The weight of that last class lecture on predictive morbidity rested squarely on her head right now, and she wanted to shake it off. Her face felt like a solid wall holding back a flood of emotions. She decided to give a clear textbook definition first to pass it off as quickly as possible.

"In the last five years, they perfected several tests with 92% accuracy that can predict if a person is within weeks, even days of final morbidity."

"I can read that on my tablet, what else do you know? How do people use that knowledge?

Has that ever been part of your internships, testing people for expiration dates?"

Alvi resisted throwing something at her sister, but she intended to keep the high moral ground as long as possible here. Crossing her arms, she stared back. "No, I am not a medical person; you know that. Advanced elders have episodes, and they do not return from the hospital. I have nothing to do with that. Anyway, they were still talking about a refined reliable concept being a future possibility. It was not perfected yet and even if it was, who and or what would people do with that knowledge?"

"Do you want to know?" said Maya.

CHAPTER 43

The longer she listened to the music, the more familiar it became. Nevertheless, Ella couldn't pinpoint where or when she had heard it before. Other than being a lively classical piece, there were no other voices or other noises coming from behind the curtain. Ella toyed with the idea of invading a private party. Maybe this is where the rich folk hung out. She had climbed up this far up from the lower decks, but she was supposed to be meeting with Riley right now.

From behind her, Ella heard a soft voice.

"Excuse me; sorry, I am late for my shift. If you need a visitor's pass, hold on a moment, and I will get that for you."

Ella turned to see a somewhat younger woman wearing a very colorful caftan. Her nametag had Doula Society above her picture. As she stepped out of the woman's way, the curtain slid to the right. She could see a look of relief on the face of the woman from behind the curtain. The woman owned a practiced and perpetual smile.

"Thank goodness; you are here early, I need to take bed 6 down, bed 5 is asleep but has been alert, and bed 4 is a bit agitated. The rest need more attention than I can give them. It has been a long shift."

Without any hesitation, the woman drew the rest of the heavy curtain back. The woman in the caftan gestured to Ella to wait just inside the curtain. In the fading light across the small deck sat a half dozen hospital like beds on wheels. Their occupants were a row of gray and white haired heads covered up to their chins in soft pastel blankets. Most had the look of ancient parchment ready to crumble and blow away with the wind. Some were half-upright peeking out towards the ocean while others were lying there. The two women walked over to the far side as she heard, "I will take bed 6 down right now. Check on the others. I will be back as soon as I can."

Ella searched for the word in her mind; she knew of birth doulas back then. They were to help focus on the mother while the medical staff concentrated on the baby being born. Since the new fertility with every birth a triumph to continue humanity, she thought the need for them had faded. Young people were now given multiple services in the full-court press for procreation through early childhood care. She realized she was witnessing the other end of that care spectrum – death doulas.

Ella realized what Riley had failed to do back at the dock was to sort sinister from purposeful. Nobody here was kicking up his or her heels, but here was a spirit of gentle compassion. This arrangement was simply a chance to breathe their last outside of a hospital or a small living space. There were some protective barriers like giant paneled windows that could be moved, but it was mostly open now to the fading sunshine. It reminded her of a botanical conservatory, but the elders were the ones looking out not in. The plant and topiary and floral arrangements were probably fake but of a quality to add to the illusion of being in a well-maintained garden with orchestral accompaniment. Ella found herself drawn forward deeper into the space by a sense of practical reverence. As when she stood in front of the glassed in cherry tree back home, she was focused not on death but on the lingering life that was here. She stopped at the first bed closest to the curtain. The doula was still standing by the bed at the far end. She could disappear the minute the doula left her sight. She had no right to be here, yet she felt her mind, and her spirit fusing together in a moment of peace. Fate for once had brought her where she was supposed to be.

She became aware of the eyes of the woman in the bed closest to her. They were following her. A thin speckled arm came out from below the soft pink blanket and seemed to levitate of its own will. Ella extended her arm down to the woman as she let herself sink in the canvas chair beside the bed. She touched the woman's hand at first treating it like a twig that could snap. Then she felt a warm, supple grip wrap around her fingers. Clouded blue eyes peered up from a frame of wispy white hair. There was no fear, no urgency.

Ella ceded her planned escape and sat forward in the chair. She could do this part; hold someone's hand, to let her know she was not alone. Years ago, she had been taught that strength was not something you give away or have taken from you, that it flowed in both directions. Ella waited, but nothing came from the thin lips except the sound of shallow breathing. What was there to say? She qualified as an intruder, yet she was welcome. A glow of inner peace surrounded this woman, and she would do nothing to disrupt it. Being there was all that the woman sought. Ella relaxed as she saw the barest hint of a smile.

She wasn't supposed to be in this place, but no one was pushing her out. She looked over at the doula, leaning over the person on the end bed, taking a pulse. She pressed a beeper on her belt, kicked off the emergency brake, and pushed the bed back down the far side as two male attendants came quickly towards her. The three of them took their places at the rolling bedside, and they headed through a swinging door.

Ella shivered with the thought. This person was very close to their end and needed more attention. She had filled out a living will. It was like a final bucket list of what you don't want done to you as death tries to steal you away.

CHAPTER 44

Riley reached the top of the long curving staircase and gave out a small shout as she saw how far up she had come. She caught her breath and relished the feeling of being looser in her knees and hip joints. To save time she could have taken the elevator but this was a better choice. Tess's leftover patches were working their magic on her whole system. She had to admit; maybe the Institute's expertise was worth something. For once, she was the beneficiary of someone else's misfortune instead of the other way around. She would take these patches to a doctor and demand an equivalent. Feeling less like a piece of damaged goods that would be discarded, she could deal better with her paranoia as her mind focused on what she needed to do. She should use this energy and time to help Ella. As she looked back to the last few weeks, there was no pride in what she had done. She could only excuse it as well-intentioned ignorance. Her interactions with Ella had taken one of the most positive people she ever knew and used her rantings to wear her down to a bundle of self-doubt. At every turn, she yanked the trust right out from under her.

Years ago, this same woman friended her through a bad episode and stopped her from taking a fatal step. Ella's actions had helped her throw the pills away and steer her towards a predictable life in an unpredictable time. She couldn't just leave her here. By early tomorrow morning, she should have orders to be at the airport for military transport to Denmark with the rest of the A level coding team. Once they got weather clearance, they would leave in a matter of hours. Now that Ella was not returning texts, she had to find her.

Over at the railing, she scanned the other ships at the dock. All was calm even out to the original gulf. She had tried to board this ship that day. How many elders had they put on this ship back near home and from other cities? They were a thousand miles plus away. The only tourist like people she saw getting on board the vessel was the younger couples. Families relocating had been living on the two lower decks, but most had disembarked even as the IT people got on.

She now knew it was safe for Ella to stay on the ship; but they did not have much time to deal with what happened next. For once, she needed to feel her way out of this. Her time with Grayson had mirrored a reflection of her hard ass attitude, and she had found it difficult to watch. If everything always turned to crap, why bother trying to save the day. Stop damning the establishment and think like there was a future. Her old habits got her nowhere; she needed to reinvent her attitude if only for Ella's sake. Grayson had planted his own words in her brain,

"You have to know what your brand of hope is made of and whether you can keep buying into it."

Maybe she could handle this pull towards something positive. She kept climbing the stairs two at a time, going down and around each deck. She turned the corner on another deck and passed the gym and spa area — no sign of Grayson, only a handful of crewmembers working in service areas, somehow finding him seemed futile while they were still sitting in the harbor. Maybe he was not even on the board, and that was why he did not give her a cell number. It could all be just a game to him. The ship seemed now more like a tourist attraction and less like an ocean liner with a covert mission. What seemed so sinister to her weeks ago had a different feel now, hearing the laughter and the high spirits of the passengers. As with the train ride, people were finding simple pleasure in being around others.

Pressing forward against the railing for a quick break, she took in the crowded rebuilt port city with all its weather fortifications. The lines of people getting on and off the ship and others never seemed to stop. She bounced over to the other side of the deck to take in the sight of the open ocean. The grayscale tone of the water was far from the iconic Caribbean blues and greens of days past. Yet it somehow held a sense of majesty and a call to adventure. Up here on the upper decks and not crammed below with so many souls, it felt different from the colony and the train. It was a lot of humanity to handle at one time, but maybe she could get used to it.

Riley looked at her cell again and saw an earlier message unanswered. She had asked Ella to meet her in one of the eating areas on Deck 6. Back inside, she stood at the elevator and studied the diagram again. There were multiple dining rooms. She checked her ticket to figure out where she was supposed to be. The ship's schematic caught her attention again. That same space on the top deck was like a void. Nothing marked to indicate its function.

Crashing that secret space was her goal when she had left the cabin. Maybe she should leave it alone for once.

She wanted to find Ella for two reasons, the second of which was the hope that Ella would tell her what to think. She needed a compass, not a moral one, rather a big arrow pointing towards something more like happiness. For now, the truth seemed to be handing her a good deal. She had the right to look forward to the crazy trip in a flying air fortress across a storm challenged ocean. Maybe she would end up seeing if life was so perfect in another so-ciety where things were right before the rest of the world was wrong. With or without Ella or this interesting stranger, she was finding her way out of the maze.

CHAPTER 45

Ella slid her key fob as she knocked on their cabin door. No Riley. Her stomach reminded her that it was past dinnertime. Her last text was still stuck in send, delivery delayed. This ship had odd pockets where your devices worked but not in others. Not a great thing for an IT conference but it was what they had. Maybe she should sit here for a while. Her options were more exciting than a few days ago. She scanned her email for any SOS from Tess. All she had sent yesterday was a smile emoji saying, "Wish you were here even though you do not want to be — feeling well. Their intervention cure is working. I will be returning on the coast train soon."

She had slipped away up top when other visitors had showed up. Again, no one questioned her presence. It seemed being dressed like a free spirit in her sister's blouse was more of a nametag than her ID. The quick descent back down all the stairs had left her breathless not so much from the exercise but from the feeling of peace she left there. Now she could inform Riley that all her suspicions were unwarranted. There were no prisoners on this ghost ship, only travelers on a final journey.

Mattie had given her a ticket for the party train back to the Colony that was valid for another two weeks plus accommodations onshore. If the company did not choose Riley for the long trip, she had the choice to stay here and fudge the expertise that she needed to pass as Riley's assistant for the rest of the regular conference. Then they could return together. If Riley were chosen for the long trip to the servers in Denmark, she would wish her well knowing her friend might never come back. Another choice was brewing in her head and making its way through her heart. There was no such thing as help wanted signs or internet listings to say older workers wanted here. How much money would it take to live without her housing subsidy? There was money in her asset account that would keep her in room and board until she figured something out.

She did not feel like a stranger in a strange land. She was simply an older version of her younger self that wanted more out of life even as her years were heading towards past due. Her excellent health was hers, and her need to stay connected stronger than ever after the train ride. The idea of starting all over again must be insane to others. Here in the land of changing temperatures and transit populations, maybe she could do something worthwhile. For the dozen-plus years she had been alone, she always prided herself on being her own person. New Florida was one of the crazy climate states, two-thirds of its former size and twice its population. Here the worst of climate terror had been the catalyst for the minds of engineers to come up with solutions from the beginning. Her protected little part of the world and her private little unit seemed very far away. Ella visualized the single curated cherry tree at the community center, something to be marveled at but only as an exception to the rule of nature. That tree was not supposed to exist but, to everyone's delight, it did. She was no longer a spectacle of the Institute, the extra years she owned for whatever reason, were hers to fill.

On the upper deck earlier, when the second doula saw her at the woman's bed holding her hand she promptly produced a CCR visitor badge. Ella did not say anything to the contrary. She could go back up behind the embossed curtain tonight or tomorrow if she wanted. Somehow, in embracing the realities of death, maybe she was deciding what to do with the rest of her life.

CHAPTER 46

Alvi hovered a while longer over her sister relishing her I know more than you do moment. Maya was prepared to listen to what she had to say. She explained that her professors had not laid out any grand scheme with predictive algorithms. Elders without severe medical complications that needed extensive medical support could choose where they wanted to be when death finally came for them. As far as she knew, no one was being hustled off to be harvested. Such knowledge would be valuable. People could choose to make reconciliations or to sort out that last bit of their lives.

The reality of her responsibilities kicked back to Alvi. What she did in her everyday duties mattered to keep people independent for as long as possible. Maya was calling it the silver thread society or something after an ancient Greek goddess who decided when to cut the thread of life. They suspected this was where their parents were right now, attending to their aunt's last wishes.

"Well, I guess we have to follow the trail in front of us no matter what you promised mom."

Alvi felt the resentment rising again. Maya was pushing to make her story copy first priority. As a journalist, she was still scratching for another angle to the story.

"This Klotho Society is as close to a modern-day secret death society as you can get." Alvi listened as Maya explained the need to expose to the public who was really benefiting from this whole scenario of coddled death by the seaside or wherever people choose to go.

Her editors had placed several reporters in the field on a national basis, but Maya sat within a few blocks of living proof of its existence. It was hard to blame her sister for wanting to be ahead of everyone else, but this was a private family matter. She knew Maya would take advantage and get the story even at the emotional expense of violating her parents and their aunt's wishes. All they had from their mother was a promise to call back and let them know when they were to join them for a memorial service.

Alvi slipped back to the lost feelings of an eight-year-old. If too many rules were broken, chaos happened. Yes, the truth mattered, but many things could also be destroyed by letting Maya do the wrong thing right now. She could make a very private moment for their family a public spectacle.

Maya was back on the cell, making promises to scoop the story. Her editor had given her a solid idea where her parents and their aunt must be. This time Alvi could hear ..." somewhere on the older ship at the end of the harbor." Maya started barking orders at her again.

"All we have to do is get on that ship. I have press credentials and..."

Alvi stopped her mid-sentence.

"There are just too many rules being broken here."

Maya waved her Press pass.

"What about defining the truth and not spreading lies?"

Alvi shuddered. Her sister's use of the word truth was always like flashing a warning message across her consciousness; you must always seek the truth.

CHAPTER 47

Riley had checked her work messages just a few minutes ago and looked for final confirmation on her travel. She was ranked high on the A team list but no last sign off yet. Her project boss continued to make staffing decisions on the fly as conditions were changing with the cyber threat of the moment. She heard the beep of another message – finally an answer. She was going, but no coding assistants were authorized beyond a few days to stay on the ship to finish some ancillary work. Most of her work peers would be traveling back to their home offices. She needed to let Ella know she was definitely out of the full trip to Denmark; she typed in another text but still no delivery. Now she had to convince Ella to take a quick vacation and return home. If after the assignment, she decided to immigrate to Denmark with her valued skill set that would be her own choice. She had chased her conspiracy theories down here where inland water was the greatest threat. For once, she had to stop fighting and win something for herself. After leading Ella down a scary path, she now wanted to push her back the other way to the real safety of the Colony. Her conspiracy theories seemed like a sticky web that was serving no one.

Finally, a text returned from Ella: Heading to the top deck, can't meet you now, will explain later. Riley texted back: Must talk to you right now, I have a final answer. There was no reply. That was all Riley needed. She bolted straight out to the elevator and pushed the up button. When it did not respond, she went to the stairs on the other side of the boat. For once, she was not heading off with a head of steam to defend or expose something. All she wanted right now was to help Ella make the right decision. Ella had been the patient understanding friend when she lost her peer group. Almost a generation apart, Ella did not judge her attitude, her hair, and tattoos, her dark thoughts. Now she tried to gather her best listening skills for what they were worth and prepare to throw them back the other way. Earlier Ella hinted at staying in this crazy New Florida and not going back, selling her unit, and just letting things happen. It was a different feeling – she was jealous.

Ella seemed to have lost her fear.

CHAPTER 48

Ella knew where she wanted to be, back up on the top deck. Stepping off the elevator on the deck below, she started up the last staircase. There must be a separate elevator to get all the way up, but it was not easy to figure out where it was. This time she would enter from the other side of the deck. As she approached, a security guard was standing by the same curtain. She waved the pass the doula had given her earlier, and he held back the curtain. This side was somewhat different; she had to cross past the entrance to what looked like a clinical space.

The sun was ready to dip below the hazy horizon to end the day. The surprising spectacle of changing color and cloud formations distracted her for a moment. She allowed herself a moment at the railing — not a postcard sunset but worthy of more than a glance.

As she moved quietly across the deck and beyond what looked like a nurse's station, she heard her name. "Ms. Ella?"

Turning towards the center, Ella scanned the few beds still on deck. A silver-white head with a ponytail winding its way across his pillow was smiling at her.

"Harold?" she tried to control her voice in a harsh whisper. She took the few short steps to his bed. Tears were brimming around his soft gray eyes. The outline of his body under the covers moved ever so slightly towards her. A side chair was there. She pulled it close and said nothing at first. The shadows of the evening were falling over both of them, each trying to smile but staying silent. Time was standing still as they absorbed the gravity of this encounter. Ella knew they would soon get past the casual greeting and a pleasantry or two that was their history. They would go slowly like moving across thin ice.

She decided it would be best first to resume their usual banter from the few times she had spoken to him.

"I get to ask this time, what is a nice guy like you doing in a place like this?" He pushed his head back with effort and puffed out a slight laugh.

"This is what becomes of old men who live alone. I have passed my crescendo, and I am waiting for the end."

Ella put her hands in her lap. This was different from sitting with the sweet stranger just a while ago. She and Harold had some history even if all it amounted to was that she knew how isolated he had chosen to be. Better to let him take the lead as to what her purpose would be here. He had always managed to be the bare minimum of sociable without offending anyone. Ella understood his perspective, a true hermit of old age. Right now, she sat in the midst of many pieces of fate falling together.

"I thought I might make it out to the open ocean again, but they are not sure, they got this thing down to a science you know." His head moved to look again out at the view of the water meeting the sky and then back.

Ella quickly considered and dismissed the idea that the Longevity Institute had anything to do with this. It all seemed contrary to their mission. Everything the Institute did was to research and solve the puzzle of how to live as long as possible. They never touched the obvious that somehow there was always a finale.

Harold's voice sounded both hollow and harsh at the same time.

"Can I ask something of you?"

He slid his arm out from under the thin blanket and showed her his medical bracelet.

"Could you copy down these two numbers and make sure that my grandnephew has it to call? I am trusting that my assets will be disposed of correctly as I asked, but it would make me feel so much better."

Ella met the gravity of Harold's simple request with a single nod. She put the name of the Klotho society contact person and an account number in her cell.

"I promise I will get this to him. I met him at least once."

Then there came another long silence. Harold was scanning the horizon.

"They will be coming soon. I am insisting they leave me up here as long as possible. It is probably my last time on deck, hoping for a decent sunset at least."

Again, Ella fought for what to say, and then she realized her purpose today was merely to listen and to reflect what feelings Harold had at this moment. Maybe someone who chose to stay so isolated might not be a self-centered person, just content in his solitude. What his life meant to him was his own legacy.

He turned again to face her as best he could. His breathing was shallow, yet his sense of peace and the absence of fear were somehow reassuring even in the absolute stillness. She wondered if he was hearing his fine music in his head.

"Do I get to give a younger woman a piece of advice?"

Ella pulled her chair closer. He gazed directly at her with mischief in his eyes for the briefest moment.

"Remember the famous physicist that Hawking fellow who said, don't look down at your feet, but rather up to the stars? I spent way too much time doing the first part and not the second. Do not waste any of the time you have left. You are a fine woman."

He took another raspy breath. His words landed softly.

"Fight for it. You deserve more out of this life."

Ella felt tenderness and enthusiasm roll over her and take hold. The tears were fighting their way out now. Moving forward again, she placed her hand next to his. It was as if all of him was melting into the mattress and she could not bring him back. She smiled and managed to give him a wink. She did not want to cry. He had given her an elegant gift, and she wanted to receive it with grace.

He started to talk about past times but lost his voice and just nodded at her. Ella noticed an attendant coming towards them. As he got closer, she spotted the tattoo on his forearm. Her eyes went to his nametag.

"Well hello, Grayson, so you are Riley's mystery man." He almost jumped backward but composed himself as he read her visitor nametag.

"Is she here?"

"Yes, I think she is headed up here on the port side. I am supposed to meet her just outside the other curtain."

"I should take him down. It is getting late. He is too weak to be left alone."

"I can stay with him. He wants to see the sunset or maybe the stars come out."

Grayson walked around in front and asked him if he understood. Harold managed a slight nod. He turned to Ella and gave her Harold's alert fob. "If he shows signs of discomfort, just let us know, and we will be here to assist him."

She watched Grayson move across the deck to the other side. As she looked back at Harold, his eyelids were gently twitching. She spoke softly to let him know she would stay beside him. A thin droll smile emerged on his lips. Ella inhaled some of the sea air and sat back in the shallow depth of the chair anchoring herself for what was to come. She did not want to be anywhere else right now. Here she was at another person's ending still relishing her thoughts of a new beginning. She would have to do battle with this odd mix of feelings later. That was not important now. Harold could have only hours left in his long life, and she would preserve his quiet resolve the best she could. Fear was not intruding here.

EPILOGUE

Ella counted the train cars from the front engine. She walked right up to the ticket taker. He saw what she had in her hands and tipped his hat; this was a familiar ritual.

"The train will be leaving in 15 minutes."

"I will just be 10."

She pulled herself up the train steps and turned left. Halfway down the aisle, she recognized the back of two heads together, one old - one young. She squeezed her way past the boarding passengers. Their faces drooped with disappointment. They were going back home; their adventure was over.

"Hey," she said as she tapped Tess on the shoulder. Ella swung the cellophane wrapper with the orchid plant to the space between them.

Tess greeted her friend with a wide smile and reached out to take her hand. Ella pulled forward so she could look directly at both Tess and Alvi. There was a lively animation of emotions still playing across the young woman's face. Add to that a soft glow of confidence.

"How are you doing Alvi? It has been quite a week for you."

Ella had watched Alvi deal with a trifecta of freaking out over last night's events, seeing Harold, Riley, and Ella all there in death's waiting room had put the young woman into emotional overload. She had triumphed, as she understood that none of this was an error on her part. Before their eyes, Alvi had scolded her sister, admonished her parents, and still had been able to deal peacefully with a death in her own family. Ella had watched the regimented young woman absorb all that had happened the night before and come to terms with their individual decisions. She had learned the lesson that her level of vigilance came at a cost to her. No one person or movement was going to change the past or guarantee the future.

Alvi simply nodded, smiled, and held her aunt's orchid closer to her. "I guess I got to realize that things need to work themselves out, I can't always have control, and that no one expects me to."

Ella glanced down at the two silk orchid plants sitting next to each other. Each had a small silver twisted vial that held part of the liquefied remains. The markings of two plants were different, one with pinks dots like brush strokes, the other with purples splotches. They were separate history maps of two very different lives that somehow ended in the same place.

Ella held out a small envelope. "This is a note from me to Harold's relative. I made a promise, and I am sure you will follow through with it." Alvi proudly took the envelope and put it in her bag.

"Not to worry, my sister's investigative team says the Klotho Society is basically legit, a business that is giving people what they want. All the assets minus their stated fees have been going back to the family since they started the society. As it keeps growing, it won't be such a secret anymore. I am sure Colin will appreciate having part of Harold's remains as well."

"Is Riley off on her long trip?"

"Yes, I just saw her off. She attended the service for Harold with me this morning. Grayson turned out to be also in charge of the crematorium as well. They are both still deciding if having a relationship is worth the risk of it falling apart. He came this morning to the airport to have a few words with her before she was off to her adventure in Denmark."

"Everyone is going in different directions," said Tess.

"What is important," said Ella," is that we are all going in our own directions. I will be in touch."

She leaned in to give Tess a big hug as she heard the shrill siren for departure. They would not lose touch again.

Back down on the train platform, Ella went inside the station and went straight for the lockers. She pulled out her single small bag, packed for a new lifetime. Her fingers fished around in the bottom until she found her Life-Bit. It was still flickering with information, intruding into her life even though she had not worn it since yesterday. Looking around, she spotted a solar trash compactor. Holding it up like a dead rodent, she dropped it in. The crunching whirring sound was very reassuring. Her health history was still out there, but for now, she could imagine that a metal bird of prey was swallowing up all that analysis.

These last months of feeling the victim, the target of exploitation had taken its toll. That gnawing sense of fear, of wanting to hide and ask no more of life was drowning in the bustling life that was now around her. She would play with a new plan to seed her future. Yes, this land was bruised and beaten, but it still had a future, and so did she.

She owned her power to change things. The short time she had spent with the woman on the top deck was both peaceful and profound. By her mere presence, she brought comfort to someone ready to depart this crazy world. Ella recognized a feeling of envy; the woman was getting what she wanted - a gentle passing - a truce with death- without a struggle. The woman's smile said to her I have no regrets. Harold had ended his symphony with a conductor's touch. Maybe, in the end, you have to push fear away and only let go.

Her immediate future was not certain. She made contact with the Doula Society, and they had encouraged her to try the next training session as both a death and a birth doula. She would travel wherever the centers needed extra help. The weather would always be a challenge; the food still less than you wanted, but the rewards were real. Maybe her gift would be in sharing her positive spirit in watching life begin as well as emptying out.

As to her own years, she was counting differently now. She was the one to carry her truth and no one else's, and she still had time for it to grow into something better.

* * *

L.I.F.E. Database Control Center – 6.1.2039 –
    10:33 AM EST
Location; Lakewood Florida
Subject ED 540 752-O
Bio-Genome Harvest Project: Priority: 4 F
    status
Full voluntary withdrawal of monitoring:
    Send message:

TECH #1

"This one is taking herself totally off the grid even for basic information exchange."
TECH #2

"We have confirmation of irretrievable bio value, so it does not matter."
TECH#1

"Her basic longevity prediction is 21-27 years remaining in health span barring natural disasters."
TECH #2

"Terminate all Secondary Tracking methods. She is on her own."
TECH#1

"Want to put in a long-term bet on estimated year of death?"
TECH#2

"No, she could outlast her own stats. Hope is a powerful booster of its own."

THE END

GLOSSARY OF FACT AND FICTION

AOTT: And All of This is True, News crawl/ chyron scrolling at the bottom of the screen to certify that the news being presented is not false information

AWE: An acute weather event requiring sheltering in place because of severe conditions.

BCE: Bureau of Culture and Entertainment, archives video and audio of all the sights and sounds from previous decades.

CCR: The closest concerned relative or friend designated for purposes of keeping contact with elderly citizens living on their own.

CLIMATE COLONY: Housing communities rebuilt to withstand harsh climate and provide resources to citizens.

C3: Constant Cylinder Companion; future generation of remote voice interface.

CNN: Caucasian Nationalist Nation

DFF SCORE: Anticipated years and days of aging well based on longevity research.

ELDER ORPHAN: A medical term for aged individuals who are socially or physically isolated, without an available known family member, designated surrogate, or caregiver.

KLOTHO SOCIETY: Organization that uses available complex AI algorithms to predict approximate time of death for elders and offers death trip packages complete with care and comfort for your final time.

L.I.F.E. Database: Longevity Institute's control center for research to extend the average life span and health span. L.I.F.E. stands for Longevity Improvement Forensic Experiments.

LIFE BIT: A variation of fitness/activity monitor for Longevity Institute members that monitor all their functions and tracks their location 24/7

NDC: National Disease Control Center is responsible for eradicating all known medical problems from the population.

SHH: Self Health Help advice for citizens on how to stay healthy longer.

TELOMERES: Found on the tips of our DNA. Recent NIH studies indicate that telomere length, can be affected by various lifestyle factors and alter the pace of aging and the onset of age-associated diseases.

UBI: Universal basic income is a model for providing all citizens of a country or other geographic area with a given sum of income.

ACKNOWLEDGEMENTS

The great books I have read over the years have all contributed to my effort to tell a worthwhile story. Books like Rachel Carson's *Silent Spring* that made me an early cli-fi watcher back in 9th grade. Margaret Atwood's novels showed me over the years what real speculative fiction is all about. Her recent short "Torching the Dusties" from *Stone Mattress: Nine Wicked Tales* helped produce the worry beads of my blogs on aging and push me over into the fiction arena.

I am grateful for all the online resources available to aspiring writers. From the Jerry Jenkins Writers Guild, I learned how to trigger the theater of the reader's mind. From the illustrious blogs and Facebook posts of K.M. Weiland at Helping Writers Become Authors, I found a steady stream of valued guidance. Jane Friedman is truly the guru of online writing resources.

In my real world off the computer, I want to first thank my lifelong friend Meg for her early encouragement to keep going on my project. Also, I want to give a shout out to the members of the Western MD Writers Group and Frederick Writers Salon, with a special nod to Barbara Harrison for her enlightened support.

I am forever grateful to my editors Sharon Umbaugh of the Writers Reader and Kelly Magee, and Allison Erin Wright of Wright Editing for their professional insight and expertise.

ABOUT THE AUTHOR

M.K. Wark has been blogging and teaching about the realities of aging for the last few years. This debut novel is a byproduct of trying to make sense of it all. Always a futurist speculating on what comes next, she has launched SilverReads, an indie imprint for future-forward fiction geared towards older adults.

She lives in Frederick, Maryland where she still believes in gardening.

Find out more at:

https://silverreads.com
https://www.facebook.
com/M-K-Wark-Author
Blog: https://waystostay.org